*The Water Babies*

This edition published 1994 by Wordsworth Editions Ltd,
Cumberland House, Crib Street, Ware, Hertfordshire SG12 9ET.

ISBN 1-85326-148-3

Printed and bound in Denmark by Nørhaven.

The paper in this book is produced from pure wood
pulp, without the use of chlorine or any other substance
harmful to the environment. The energy used in its
production consists almost entirely of hydroelectricity
and heat generated from waste materials, thereby
conserving fossil fuels and contributing little to the
greenhouse effect.

# THE WATER-BABIES

## A FAIRY TALE
## FOR A LAND-BABY

" I heard a thousand blended notes,
    While in a grove I sate reclined ;
In that sweet mood when pleasant thoughts
    Bring sad thoughts to the mind.

" To her fair works did Nature link
    The human soul that through me ran ;
And much it grieved my heart to think,
    What man has made of man."

WORDSWORTH.

# CHAPTER I

ONCE upon a time there was a little chimney-sweep, and his name was Tom. That is a short name, and you have heard it before, so you will not have much trouble in remembering it. He lived in a great town in the North country, where there were plenty of chimneys to sweep, and plenty of money for Tom to earn and his master to spend. He could not read nor write, and did not care to do either; and he never washed himself, for there was no water up the court where he lived. He had never been taught to say his prayers. He never had heard of God, or of Christ, except in words which you never have heard, and which it would have been well if he had never heard. He cried half his time, and laughed the other half. He cried when he had to climb the dark flues, rubbing his poor knees and elbows raw; and when the soot got into his eyes, which it did every day in the week; and when his master beat him, which he did every day in the week; and when he had not enough to eat, which happened every day in the week likewise. And he laughed the other half of the day, when he was tossing halfpennies with the other boys, or playing leap-frog over the posts, or bowling stones at the horses' legs as they trotted by, which last was excellent fun, when there was a wall at hand behind which to hide. As for chimney-sweeping, and being hungry, and being beaten, he took all that for the way of the world, like the rain and snow and thunder, and stood manfully with his back to it till it was over, as his old donkey did to a hail-storm; and then shook his ears and was as jolly as ever; and thought of the fine times coming, when he would be a man, and a master sweep, and sit in the public-house with a quart of beer and a long pipe, and play cards for silver money, and wear velveteens and ankle-jacks, and keep a white bull-dog with one grey ear, and carry her puppies in his pocket, just like a man. And he would have apprentices, one, two, three, if he could. How he would bully them, and knock them about, just as his master did to him; and make them carry home the soot sacks, while he rode before them on his donkey, with a pipe in his mouth and a flower in his button-hole, like a king at the head of his army. Yes, there were good times coming; and, when his master let him have a pull at the leavings of his beer, Tom was the jolliest boy in the whole town.

One day a smart little groom rode into the court where Tom lived. Tom was just hiding behind a wall, to heave half a brick at his horse's legs, as is the custom of that country when they welcome strangers; but the groom saw him, and halloed to him to know where Mr. Grimes, the chimney-sweep, lived. Now, Mr. Grimes was Tom's own master, and Tom was a good man of business, and always civil to customers, so he put the half-brick down quietly behind the wall, and proceeded to take orders.

Mr. Grimes was to come up next morning to Sir John Harthover's, at the Place, for his old chimney - sweep was gone to prison, and the chimneys wanted sweeping. And so he rode away, not giving Tom time to ask what the sweep had gone to prison for, which was a matter of interest to Tom, as he had been in prison once or twice himself. Moreover, the groom looked so very neat and clean, with his drab gaiters, drab breeches, drab jacket, snow-white tie with a smart pin in it, and clean round ruddy face, that Tom was offended and disgusted at his appearance, and considered him a stuck-up fellow, who gave himself airs because he wore smart clothes, and other people paid for them; and went behind the wall to fetch the half-brick after all ; but did not, remembering that he had come in the way of business, and was, as it were, under a flag of truce.

His master was so delighted at his new customer that he knocked Tom down out of hand, and drank more beer that night than he usually did in two, in order to be sure of getting up in time next morning; for the more a man's head aches when he wakes, the more glad he is to turn out, and have a breath of fresh air. And, when he did get up at four the next morning, he knocked Tom

down again, in order to teach him (as young
gentlemen used to be taught at public schools)
that he must be an extra good boy that day, as
they were going to a very great house, and might
make a very good thing of it, if they could but
give satisfaction.

And Tom thought so likewise, and, indeed,
would have done and behaved his best, even without being knocked down.  For, of all places upon
earth, Harthover Place (which he had never seen)
was the most wonderful, and, of all men on earth,
Sir John (whom he had seen, having been sent to
gaol by him twice) was the most awful.

Harthover Place was really a grand place, even
for the rich North country; with a house so large
that in the frame-breaking riots, which Tom could
just remember, the Duke of Wellington, and ten
thousand soldiers to match, were easily housed
therein; at least, so Tom believed; with a park
full of deer, which Tom believed to be monsters
who were in the habit of eating children; with
miles of game-preserves, in which Mr. Grimes
and the collier lads poached at times, on which
occasions Tom saw pheasants, and wondered what
they tasted like; with a noble salmon-river, in
which Mr. Grimes and his friends would have
liked to poach; but then they must have got into
cold water, and that they did not like at all.  In
short, Harthover was a grand place, and Sir John
a grand old man, whom even Mr. Grimes respected;
for not only could he send Mr. Grimes to prison
when he deserved it, as he did once or twice a

week; not only did he own all the land about for miles; not only was he a jolly, honest, sensible squire, as ever kept a pack of hounds, who would do what he thought right by his neighbours, as well as get what he thought right for himself; but, what was more, he weighed full fifteen stone, was nobody knew how many inches round the chest, and could have thrashed Mr. Grimes himself in fair fight, which very few folk round there could do, and which, my dear little boy, would not have been right for him to do, as a great many things are not which one both can do, and would like very much to do.  So Mr. Grimes touched his hat to him when he rode through the town, and called him a "buirdly awd chap," and his young ladies "gradely lasses," which are two high compliments in the North country; and thought that that made up for his poaching Sir John's pheasants; whereby you may perceive that Mr. Grimes had not been to a properly-inspected Government National School.

Now, I dare say, you never got up at three o'clock on a midsummer morning.  Some people get up then because they want to catch salmon; and some because they want to climb Alps; and a great many more because they must, like Tom. But, I assure you, that three o'clock on a midsummer morning is the pleasantest time of all the twenty-four hours, and all the three hundred and sixty-five days; and why every one does not get up then, I never could tell, save that they are all determined to spoil their nerves and their complexions by doing all night what they might just as well do all day. But Tom, instead of going out to dinner at half-past eight at night, and to a ball at ten, and finishing off somewhere between twelve and four, went to bed at seven, when his master went to the public-house, and slept like a dead pig; for which reason he was as piert as a game-cock (who always gets up early to wake the maids), and just ready to get up when the fine gentlemen and ladies were just ready to go to bed.

So he and his master set out; Grimes rode the donkey in front, and Tom and the brushes walked behind; out of the court, and up the street, past the closed window-shutters, and the winking weary policemen, and the roofs all shining grey in the grey dawn.

They passed through the pitmen's village, all shut up and silent now, and through the turnpike; and then they were out in the real country, and plodding along the black dusty road, between black slag walls, with no sound but the groaning and thumping of the pit-engine in the next field. But soon the road grew white, and the walls likewise; and at the wall's foot grew long grass and gay flowers, all drenched with dew; and instead of the groaning of the pit-engine, they heard the skylark saying his matins high up in the air, and the pit-bird warbling in the sedges, as he had warbled all night long.

All else was silent. For old Mrs. Earth was still fast asleep; and, like many pretty people, she looked still prettier asleep than awake. The great

elm-trees in the gold-green meadows were fast
asleep above, and the cows fast asleep beneath
them ; nay, the few clouds which were about
were fast asleep likewise, and so tired that they
had lain down on the earth to rest, in long white
flakes and bars, among the stems of the elm-trees,
and along the tops of the alders by the stream,
waiting for the sun to bid them rise and go about
their day's business in the clear blue overhead.

On they went; and Tom looked, and looked,
for he never had been so far into the country
before ; and longed to get over a gate, and pick
buttercups, and look for birds' nests in the hedge ;
but Mr. Grimes was a man of business, and would
not have heard of that.

Soon they came up with a poor Irishwoman,
trudging along with a bundle at her back.  She
had a grey shawl over her head, and a crimson
madder petticoat ; so you may be sure she came
from Galway.  She had neither shoes nor stockings,
and limped along as if she were tired and footsore ;
but she was a very tall handsome woman, with
bright grey eyes, and heavy black hair hanging
about her cheeks.  And she took Mr. Grimes'
fancy so much, that when he came alongside he
called out to her:

"This is a hard road for a gradely foot like
that.   Will ye up, lass, and ride behind me ? "

But, perhaps, she did not admire Mr. Grimes'
look and voice; for she answered quietly:

"No, thank you ; I'd sooner walk with your
little lad here."

"You may please yourself," growled Grimes, and went on smoking.

So she walked beside Tom, and talked to him, and asked him where he lived, and what he knew, and all about himself, till Tom thought he had never met such a pleasant-spoken woman. And she asked him, at last, whether he said his prayers! and seemed sad when he told her that he knew no prayers to say.

Then he asked her where she lived, and she said far away by the sea. And Tom asked her about the sea; and she told him how it rolled and roared over the rocks in winter nights, and lay still in the bright summer days, for the children to bathe and play in it; and many a story more, till Tom longed to go and see the sea, and bathe in it likewise.

At last, at the bottom of a hill, they came to a spring; not such a spring as you see here, which soaks up out of a white gravel in the bog, among red fly-catchers, and pink bottle-heath, and sweet white orchis; nor such a one as you may see, too, here, which bubbles up under the warm sandbank in the hollow lane, by the great tuft of lady ferns, and makes the sand dance reels at the bottom, day and night, all the year round; not such a spring as either of those; but a real North country lime-stone fountain, like one of those in Sicily or Greece, where the old heathen fancied the nymphs sat cooling themselves the hot summer's day, while the shepherds peeped at them from behind the bushes. Out of a low cave of rock, at the foot of a limestone crag, the great fountain rose, quelling, and bubbling, and gurgling, so clear that you could not tell where the water ended and the air began; and ran away under the road, a stream large enough to turn a mill; among blue geranium, and golden globe-flower, and wild raspberry, and the bird-cherry with its tassels of snow.

And there Grimes stopped, and looked; and Tom looked too. Tom was wondering whether anything lived in that dark cave, and came out at night to fly in the meadows. But Grimes was not wondering at all. Without a word, he got off his donkey, and clambered over the low road wall, and knelt down, and began dipping his ugly head into the spring—and very dirty he made it.

Tom was picking the flowers as fast as he could. The Irishwoman helped him, and showed him how to tie them up; and a very pretty nose-gay they had made between them. But when he saw Grimes actually wash, he stopped, quite astonished; and when Grimes had finished, and began shaking his ears to dry them, he said:

"Why, master, I never saw you do that before."

"Nor will again, most likely. 'Twasn't for cleanliness I did it, but for coolness. I'd be ashamed to want washing every week or so, like any smutty collier lad."

"I wish I might go and dip my head in," said poor little Tom. "It must be as good as putting it under the town-pump; and there is no beadle here to drive a chap away."

9

"Thou come along," said Grimes; "what dost want with washing thyself? Thou did not drink half a gallon of beer last night, like me."

"I don't care for you," said naughty Tom, and ran down to the stream, and began washing his face.

Grimes was very sulky, because the woman preferred Tom's company to his; so he dashed at him with horrid words, and tore him up from his knees, and began beating him. But Tom was accustomed to that, and got his head safe between Mr. Grimes' legs, and kicked his shins with all his might.

"Are you not ashamed of yourself, Thomas Grimes?" cried the Irishwoman over the wall.

Grimes looked up, startled at her knowing his name; but all he answered was, "No, nor never was yet"; and went on beating Tom.

"True for you. If you ever had been ashamed of yourself, you would have gone over into Vendale long ago."

"What do you know about Vendale?" shouted Grimes; but he left off beating Tom.

"I know about Vendale, and about you, too. I know, for instance, what happened in Aldermire Copse, by night, two years ago come Martinmas."

"You do?" shouted Grimes; and leaving Tom, he climbed up over the wall, and faced the woman. Tom thought he was going to strike her; but she looked him too full and fierce in the face for that.

"Yes; I was there," said the Irishwoman quietly.

"You are no Irishwoman, by your speech," said Grimes, after many bad words.

"Never mind who I am. I saw what I saw; and if you strike that boy again, I can tell what I know."

Grimes seemed quite cowed, and got on his donkey without another word.

"Stop!" said the Irishwoman. "I have one more word for you both; for you will both see me again before all is over. Those that wish to be clean, clean they will be; and those that wish to be foul, foul they will be. Remember."

And she turned away, and through a gate into the meadow. Grimes stood still a moment, like a man who had been stunned. Then he rushed after her, shouting, "You come back." But when he got into the meadow, the woman was not there.

Had she hidden away? There was no place to hide in. But Grimes looked about, and Tom also, for he was as puzzled as Grimes himself at her disappearing so suddenly; but look where they would, she was not there.

Grimes came back again, as silent as a post, for he was a little frightened; and, getting on his donkey, filled a fresh pipe, and smoked away, leaving Tom in peace.

And now they had gone three miles and more, and came to Sir John's lodge-gates.

Very grand lodges they were, with very grand iron gates and stone gate-posts, and on the top of each a most dreadful bogy, all teeth, horns, and tail, which was the crest which Sir John's ancestors wore in the Wars of the Roses; and very prudent men they were to wear it, for all their enemies must have run for their lives at the very first sight of them.

Grimes rang at the gate, and out came a keeper on the spot, and opened.

"I was told to expect thee," he said. "Now thou'lt be so good as to keep to the main avenue, and not let me find a hare or a rabbit on thee when thou comest back. I shall look sharp for one, I tell thee."

"Not if it's in the bottom of the soot-bag," quoth Grimes, and at that he laughed; and the keeper laughed and said:

"If that's thy sort, I may as well walk up with thee to the hall."

"I think thou best had. It's thy business to see after thy game, man, and not mine."

So the keeper went with them; and, to Tom's surprise, he and Grimes chatted together all the way quite pleasantly. He did not know that a keeper is only a poacher turned outside in, and a poacher a keeper turned inside out.

They walked up a great lime avenue, a full mile long, and between their stems Tom peeped trembling at the horns of the sleeping deer, which stood up among the ferns. Tom had never seen such enormous trees, and as he looked up he fancied that the blue sky rested on their heads. But he was puzzled very much by a strange murmuring noise, which followed them all the way. So much puzzled, that at last he took courage to ask the keeper what it was.

He spoke very civilly, and called him Sir, for he was horribly afraid of him, which pleased the keeper, and he told him that they were the bees about the lime flowers.

" What are bees ? " asked Tom.

" What make honey."

" What is honey? " asked Tom.

" Thou hold thy noise," said Grimes.

" Let the boy be," said the keeper. " He's a civil young chap now, and that's more than he'll be long if he bides with thee."

Grimes laughed, for he took that for a compliment.

" I wish I were a keeper," said Tom, " to live in such a beautiful place, and wear green velveteens, and have a real dog-whistle at my button, like you."

The keeper laughed; he was a kind-hearted fellow enough.

" Let well alone, lad, and ill too at times. Thy life's safer than mine at all events, eh, Mr. Grimes ? "

And Grimes laughed again, and then the two men began talking quite low.  Tom could hear, though, that it was about some poaching fight; and at last Grimes said surlily, " Hast thou anything against me ? "

" Not now."

" Then don't ask me any questions till thou hast, for I am a man of honour."

And at that they both laughed again, and thought it a very good joke.

And by this time they were come up to the great iron gates in front of the house; and Tom stared through them at the rhododendrons and azaleas, which were all in flower; and then at the house itself, and wondered how many chimneys there were in it, and how long ago it was built, and what was the man's name that built it, and whether he got much money for his job?

These last were very difficult questions to answer. For Harthover had been built at ninety different times, and in nineteen different styles, and looked as if somebody had built a whole street of houses of every imaginable shape, and then stirred them together with a spoon.

*For the attics were Anglo-Saxon.*
*The third floor Norman.*
*The second Cinque-cento.*
*The first-floor Elizabethan.*
*The right wing Pure Doric.*
*The centre Early English, with a huge portico copied from the Parthenon.*
*The left wing pure Bœotian, which the country folk admired most of all, because it was just like the new barracks in the town, only three times as big.*
*The grand staircase was copied from the Catacombs at Rome.*
*The back staircase from the Tajmahal at Agra. This was built by Sir John's great-great-great-uncle, who won, in Lord Clive's Indian Wars, plenty of*

*money, plenty of wounds, and no more taste than his betters.*

*The cellars were copied from the caves of Elephanta. The offices from the Pavilion at Brighton.*

And the rest from nothing in heaven, or earth, or under the earth.

So that Harthover House was a great puzzle to antiquarians, and a thorough Naboth's vineyard to critics, and architects, and all persons who like meddling with other men's business, and spending other men's money. So they were all setting upon poor Sir John, year after year, and trying to talk him into spending a hundred thousand pounds or so, in building, to please them and not himself. But he always put them off, like a canny North-countryman as he was. One wanted him to build a Gothic house, but he said he was no Goth ; and another to build an Elizabethan, but he said he lived under good Queen Victoria, and not good Queen Bess ; and another was bold enough to tell him that his house was ugly, but he said he lived inside it, and not outside ; and another, that there was no unity in it, but he said that that was just why he liked the old place. For he liked to see how each Sir John, and Sir Hugh, and Sir Ralph, and Sir Randal, had left his mark upon the place, each after his own taste ; and he had no more notion of disturbing his ancestors' work than of disturbing their graves. For now the house looked like a real live house, that had a history, and had grown and grown as the world grew ; and that it

was only an upstart fellow who did not know who
his own grandfather was, who would change it for
some spick and span new Gothic or Elizabethan
thing, which looked as if it had been all spawned
in a night, as mushrooms are. From which you
may collect (if you have wit enough) that Sir John
was a very sound-headed, sound-hearted squire,
and just the man to keep the country side in order,
and show good sport with his hounds.

But Tom and his master did not go in through
the great iron gates, as if they had been Dukes or
Bishops, but round the back way, and a very long
way round it was; and into a little back-door,
where the ash-boy let them in, yawning horribly;
and then in a passage the housekeeper met them,
in such a flowered chintz dressing-gown, that Tom
mistook her for My Lady herself, and she gave
Grimes solemn orders about " You will take care
of this, and take care of that," as if he was going
up the chimneys, and not Tom. And Grimes
listened, and said every now and then, under his
voice, " You'll mind that, you little beggar ? " and
Tom did mind, all at least that he could. And
then the housekeeper turned them into a grand
room, all covered up in sheets of brown paper, and
bade them begin, in a lofty and tremendous voice;
and so after a whimper or two, and a kick from his
master, into the grate Tom went, and up the
chimney, while a housemaid stayed in the room
to watch the furniture; to whom Mr. Grimes paid
many playful and chivalrous compliments, but met
with very slight encouragement in return.

How many chimneys Tom swept I cannot say; but he swept so many that he got quite tired, and puzzled too, for they were not like the town flues to which he was accustomed, but such as you would find—if you would only get up them and look, which perhaps you would not like to do—in old country-houses, large and crooked chimneys, which had been altered again and again, till they ran one into another, anastomosing (as Professor Owen would say) considerably. So Tom fairly lost his way in them; not that he cared much for that, though he was in pitchy darkness, for he was as much at home in a chimney as a mole is underground; but at last, coming down as he thought the right chimney, he came down the wrong one, and found himself standing on the hearthrug in a room the like of which he had never seen before.

Tom had never seen the like. He had never been in gentlefolks' rooms but when the carpets were all up, and the curtains down, and the furniture huddled together under a cloth, and the pictures covered with aprons and dusters; and he had often enough wondered what the rooms were like when they were all ready for the quality to sit in. And now he saw, and he thought the sight very pretty.

The room was all dressed in white,—white window-curtains, white bed-curtains, white furniture, and white walls, with just a few lines of pink here and there. The carpet was all over gay little flowers; and the walls were hung with pictures in gilt frames, which amused Tom very much. There were pictures of ladies and gentlemen, and pictures of horses and dogs.   The horses he liked; but the dogs he did not care for much, for there were no bull-dogs among them, not even a terrier. But the two pictures which took his fancy most were, one a man in long garments, with little children and their mothers round him, who was laying his hand upon the children's heads.   That was a very pretty picture, Tom thought, to hang in a lady's room.   For he could see that it was a lady's room by the dresses which lay about.

The other picture was that of a man nailed to a cross, which surprised Tom much.   He fancied that he had seen something like it in a shop-window.   But why was it there?   "Poor man," thought Tom, "and he looks so kind and quiet. But why should the lady have such a sad picture as that in her room?   Perhaps it was some kins-man of hers, who had been murdered by the savages in foreign parts, and she kept it there for a remem-brance."   And Tom felt sad, and awed, and turned to look at something else.

The next thing he saw, and that too puzzled him, was a washing-stand, with ewers and basins, and soap and brushes, and towels, and a large bath full of clean water—what a heap of things all for washing !   "She must be a very dirty lady," thought Tom, "by my master's rule, to want as much scrubbing as all that.   But she must be very cunning to put the dirt out of the way so well afterwards, for I don't see a speck about the room, not even on the very towels."

And then, looking toward the bed, he saw

that dirty lady, and held his breath with astonishment.

Under the snow-white coverlet, upon the snow-white pillow, lay the most beautiful little girl that Tom had ever seen. Her cheeks were almost as white as the pillow, and her hair was like threads of gold spread all about over the bed. She might have been as old as Tom, or maybe a year or two older; but Tom did not think of that. He thought only of her delicate skin and golden hair, and wondered whether she was a real live person, or one of the wax dolls he had seen in the shops. But when he saw her breathe, he made up his mind that she was alive, and stood staring at her, as if she had been an angel out of heaven.

No. She cannot be dirty. She never could have been dirty, thought Tom to himself. And then he thought, "And are all people like that when they are washed?" And he looked at his own wrist, and tried to rub the soot off, and wondered whether it ever would come off. "Certainly I should look much prettier then, if I grew at all like her."

And looking round, he suddenly saw, standing close to him, a little ugly, black, ragged figure, with bleared eyes and grinning white teeth. He turned on it angrily. What did such a little black ape want in that sweet young lady's room? And behold, it was himself, reflected in a great mirror, the like of which Tom had never seen before.

And Tom, for the first time in his life, found out that he was dirty; and burst into tears with shame and anger; and turned to sneak up the chimney again and hide; and upset the fender and threw the fire-irons down, with a noise as of ten thousand tin kettles tied to ten thousand mad dogs' tails.

Up jumped the little white lady in her bed, and, seeing Tom, screamed as shrill as any peacock. In rushed a stout old nurse from the next room, and seeing Tom likewise, made up her mind that he had come to rob, plunder, destroy, and burn; and dashed at him, as he lay over the fender, so fast that she caught him by the jacket.

But she did not hold him. Tom had been in a policeman's hands many a time, and out of them too, what is more; and he would have been ashamed to face his friends for ever if he had been stupid enough to be caught by an old woman; so he doubled under the good lady's arm, across the room, and out of the window in a moment.

He did not need to drop out, though he would have done so bravely enough. Nor even to let himself down a spout, which would have been an old game to him; for once he got up by a spout to the church roof, he said to take jackdaws' eggs, but the policeman said to steal lead; and, when he was seen on high, sat there till the sun got too hot, and came down by another spout, leaving the policemen to go back to the stationhouse and eat their dinners.

But all under the window spread a tree, with great leaves and sweet white flowers, almost as big as his head. It was magnolia, I suppose; but

Tom knew nothing about that, and cared less; for down the tree he went, like a cat, and across the garden lawn, and over the iron railings, and up the park towards the wood, leaving the old nurse to scream murder and fire at the window.

The under gardener, mowing, saw Tom, and threw down his scythe; caught his leg in it, and cut his shin open, whereby he kept his bed for a week; but in his hurry he never knew it, and gave chase to poor Tom. The dairymaid heard the noise, got the churn between her knees, and tumbled over it, spilling all the cream; and yet she jumped up, and gave chase to Tom. A groom cleaning Sir John's hack at the stables let him go loose, whereby he kicked himself lame in five minutes; but he ran out and gave chase to Tom. Grimes upset the soot-sack in the new-gravelled yard, and spoilt it all utterly; but he ran out and gave chase to Tom. The old steward opened the park-gate in such a hurry, that he hung up his pony's chin upon the spikes, and, for aught I know, it hangs there still; but he jumped off, and gave chase to Tom. The ploughman left his horses at the headland, and one jumped over the fence, and pulled the other into the ditch, plough and all; but he ran on, and gave chase to Tom. The keeper, who was taking a stoat out of a trap, let the stoat go, and caught his own finger; but he jumped up, and ran after Tom; and considering what he said, and how he looked, I should have been sorry for Tom if he had caught him. Sir John looked out of his study window (for he was an early old gentleman) and up at the nurse, and a marten dropped mud in his eye, so that he had at last to send for the doctor; and yet he ran out, and gave chase to Tom. The Irishwoman, too, was walking up to the house to beg,—she must have got round by some byway,—but she threw away her bundle, and gave chase to Tom likewise. Only my Lady did not give chase; for when she had put her head out of the window, her night-wig fell into the garden, and she had to ring up her lady's-maid, and send her down for it privately, which quite put her out of the running, so that she came in nowhere, and is consequently not placed.

In a word, never was there heard at Hall Place —not even when the fox was killed in the conservatory, among acres of broken glass, and tons of smashed flower-pots—such a noise, row, hubbub, babel, shindy, hullabaloo, stramash, charivari, and total contempt of dignity, repose, and order, as that day, when Grimes, gardener, the groom, the dairymaid, Sir John, the steward, the ploughman, the keeper, and the Irishwoman, all ran up the park, shouting "Stop thief," in the belief that Tom had at least a thousand pounds' worth of jewels in his empty pockets; and the very magpies and jays followed Tom up, screaking and screaming, as if he were a hunted fox, beginning to droop his brush.

And all the while poor Tom paddled up the park with his little bare feet, like a small black gorilla fleeing to the forest. Alas for him! there

was no big father gorilla therein to take his part
—to scratch out the gardener's inside with one
paw, toss the dairymaid into a tree with another,
and wrench off Sir John's head with a third, while
he cracked the keeper's skull with his teeth as
easily as if it had been a cocoa-nut or a paving-
stone.

However, Tom did not remember ever having
had a father; so he did not look for one, and
expected to have to take care of himself; while as
for running, he could keep up for a couple of miles
with any stage-coach, if there was the chance of a
copper or a cigar-end, and turn coach-wheels on
his hands and feet ten times following, which is
more than you can do. Wherefore his pursuers
found it very difficult to catch him; and we will
hope that they did not catch him at all.

Tom, of course, made for the woods. He had
never been in a wood in his life; but he was sharp
enough to know that he might hide in a bush, or
swarm up a tree, and, altogether, had more chance
there than in the open. If he had not known
that, he would have been foolisher than a mouse
or a minnow.

But when he got into the wood, he found it
a very different sort of place from what he had
fancied. He pushed into a thick cover of rhododendrons, and found himself at once caught in a
trap. The boughs laid hold of his legs and arms,
poked him in his face and his stomach, made him
shut his eyes tight (though that was no great loss,
for he could not see at best a yard before his nose);

and when he got through the rhododendrons, the hassock-grass and sedges tumbled him over, and cut his poor little fingers afterwards most spitefully ; the birches birched him as soundly as if he had been a nobleman at Eton, and over the face too (which is not fair swishing, as all brave boys will agree) ; and the lawyers tripped him up, and tore his shins as if they had sharks' teeth—which lawyers are likely enough to have.

"I must get out of this," thought Tom, "or I shall stay here till somebody comes to help me— which is just what I don't want."

But how to get out was the difficult matter. And indeed I don't think he would ever have got out at all, but have stayed there till the cock-robins covered him with leaves, if he had not suddenly run his head against a wall.

Now running your head against a wall is not pleasant, especially if it is a loose wall, with the stones all set on edge, and a sharp cornered one hits you between the eyes and makes you see all manner of beautiful stars. The stars are very beautiful, certainly ; but unfortunately they go in the twenty-thousandth part of a split second, and the pain which comes after them does not. And so Tom hurt his head ; but he was a brave boy, and did not mind that a penny. He guessed that over the wall the cover would end ; and up it he went, and over like a squirrel.

And there he was, out on the great grouse-moors, which the country folk called Harthover

Fell—heather and bog and rock, stretching away and up, up to the very sky.

Now, Tom was a cunning little fellow — as cunning as an old Exmoor stag. Why not? Though he was but ten years old, he had lived longer than most stags, and had more wits to start with into the bargain.

He knew as well as a stag that if he backed he might throw the hounds out. So the first thing he did when he was over the wall was to make the neatest double sharp to his right, and run along under the wall for nearly half a mile.

Whereby Sir John, and the keeper, and the steward, and the gardener, and the ploughman, and the dairymaid, and all the hue-and-cry together, went on ahead half a mile in the very opposite direction, and inside the wall, leaving him a mile off on the outside; while Tom heard their shouts die away in the woods and chuckled to himself merrily.

At last he came to a dip in the land, and went to the bottom of it, and then he turned bravely away from the wall and up the moor; for he knew that he had put a hill between him and his enemies, and could go on without their seeing him.

But the Irishwoman, alone of them all, had seen which way Tom went. She had kept ahead of every one the whole time; and yet she neither walked nor ran. She went along quite smoothly and gracefully, while her feet twinkled past each other so fast that you could not see which was foremost; till every one asked the other who the strange woman was; and all agreed, for want of anything better to say, that she must be in league with Tom.

But when she came to the plantation, they lost sight of her; and they could do no less. For she went quietly over the wall after Tom, and followed him wherever he went. Sir John and the rest saw no more of her; and out of sight was out of mind.

And now Tom was right away into the heather, over just such a moor as those in which you have been bred, except that there were rocks and stones lying about everywhere, and that, instead of the moor growing flat as he went upwards, it grew more and more broken and hilly, but not so rough but that little Tom could jog along well enough, and find time, too, to stare about at the strange place, which was like a new world to him.

He saw great spiders there, with crowns and crosses marked on their backs, who sat in the middle of their webs, and when they saw Tom coming, shook them so fast that they became invisible. Then he saw lizards, brown and grey and green, and thought they were snakes, and would sting him; but they were as much frightened as he, and shot away into the heath. And then, under a rock, he saw a pretty sight—a great brown, sharp-nosed creature, with a white tag to her brush, and round her four or five smutty little cubs, the funniest fellows Tom ever saw. She lay on her back, rolling about, and stretching out her legs and head and tail in the bright sunshine; and the cubs jumped over her, and ran round her, and nibbled her paws, and lugged her about by the tail; and she seemed to enjoy it mightily. But one selfish little fellow stole away from the rest to a dead crow close by, and dragged it off to hide it, though it was nearly as big as he was. Whereat all his little brothers set off after him in full cry, and saw Tom; and then all ran back, and up jumped Mrs. Vixen, and caught one up in her mouth, and the rest toddled after her, and into a dark crack in the rocks; and there was an end of the show.

And next he had a fright; for, as he scrambled up a sandy brow—whirr-poof-poof-cock-cock-kick—something went off in his face, with a most horrid noise. He thought the ground had blown up, and the end of the world come.

And when he opened his eyes (for he shut them very tight) it was only an old cock-grouse, who had been washing himself in sand, like an Arab, for want of water; and who, when Tom had all but trodden on him, jumped up with a noise like the express train, leaving his wife and children to shift for themselves, like an old coward, and went off, screaming "Cur-ru-u-uck, cur-ru-u-uck—murder, thieves, fire—cur-u-uck-cock-kick—the end of the world is come—kick-kick-cock-kick." He was always fancying that the end of the world was come, when anything happened which was farther off than the end of his own nose. But the end of the world was not come, any more than the twelfth of August was; though the old grouse-cock was quite certain of it.

So the old grouse came back to his wife and family an hour afterwards, and said solemnly, "Cock-cock-kick; my dears, the end of the world is not quite come; but I assure you it is coming the day after to-morrow—cock." But his wife had heard that so often that she knew all about it, and a little more. And, besides, she was the mother of a family, and had seven little poults to wash and feed every day; and that made her very practical, and a little sharp-tempered; so all she answered was : "Kick-kick-kick—go and catch spiders, go and catch spiders—kick."

So Tom went on and on, he hardly knew why; but he liked the great wide strange place, and the cool fresh bracing air. But he went more and more slowly as he got higher up the hill; for now the ground grew very bad indeed. Instead of soft turf and springy heather, he met great patches of flat limestone rock, just like ill-made pavements, with deep cracks between the stones and ledges, filled with ferns; so he had to hop from stone to stone, and now and then he slipped in between, and hurt his little bare toes, though they were tolerably tough ones ; but still he would go on and up, he could not tell why.

What would Tom have said if he had seen, walking over the moor behind him, the very same Irishwoman who had taken his part upon the road? But whether it was that he looked too little behind him, or whether it was that she kept out of sight behind the rocks and knolls, he never saw her, though she saw him.

And now he began to get a little hungry, and very thirsty; for he had run a long way, and the sun had risen high in heaven, and the rock was as hot as an oven, and the air danced reels over it, as it does over a limekiln, till everything round seemed quivering and melting in the glare.

But he could see nothing to eat anywhere, and still less to drink.

The heath was full of bilberries and whimberries; but they were only in flower yet, for it was June. And as for water, who can find that on the top of a limestone rock? Now and then he passed by a deep dark swallow-hole, going down into the earth, as if it was the chimney of some dwarf's house underground; and more than once, as he passed, he could hear water falling, trickling, tinkling, many many feet below. How he longed to get down to it, and cool his poor baked lips! But, brave little chimney-sweep as he was, he dared not climb down such chimneys as those.

So he went on and on, till his head spun round with the heat, and he thought he heard church-bells ringing, a long way off.

"Ah!" he thought, "where there is a church there will be houses and people; and, perhaps, some one will give me a bit and a sup." So he set off again, to look for the church; for he was sure that he heard the bells quite plain.

And in a minute more, when he looked round, he stopped again, and said, "Why, what a big place the world is!"

And so it was; for, from the top of the mountain he could see—what could he not see?

Behind him, far below, was Harthover, and the dark woods, and the shining salmon river; and on his left, far below, was the town, and the smoking chimneys of the collieries; and far, far away, the river widened to the shining sea; and little white specks, which were ships, lay on its bosom. Before him lay, spread out like a map, great plains, and farms, and villages, amid dark knots of trees. They all seemed at his very feet; but he had sense to see that they were long miles away.

And to his right rose moor after moor, hill after hill, till they faded away, blue into blue sky. But between him and those moors, and really at his very feet, lay something, to which, as soon as Tom saw it, he determined to go, for that was the place for him.

A deep, deep green and rocky valley, very narrow, and filled with wood; but through the wood, hundreds of feet below him, he could see a clear stream glance. Oh, if he could but get down to that stream! Then, by the stream, he saw the roof of a little cottage, and a little garden set out in squares and beds. And there was a tiny little red thing moving in the garden, no bigger than a fly. As Tom looked down, he saw that it was a woman in a red petticoat. Ah! perhaps she would give him something to eat. And there were the church-bells ringing again. Surely there must be a village down there. Well, nobody would know him, or what had happened at the Place.

The news could not have got there yet, even if Sir John had set all the policemen in the county after him; and he could get down there in five minutes.

Tom was quite right about the hue-and-cry not having got thither; for he had come without knowing it, the best part of ten miles from Harthover; but he was wrong about getting down in five minutes, for the cottage was more than a mile off, and a good thousand feet below.

However, down he went, like a brave little man as he was, though he was very footsore, and tired, and hungry, and thirsty; while the church-bells rang so loud, he began to think that they must be inside his own head, and the river chimed and tinkled far below; and this was the song which it sang:—

> Clear and cool, clear and cool,
> By laughing shallow, and dreaming pool;
> Cool and clear, cool and clear,
> By shining shingle, and foaming wear;
> Under the crag where the ouzel sings,
> And the ivied wall where the church-bell rings,
> Undefiled, for the undefiled;
> Play by me, bathe in me, mother and child.

> Dank and foul, dank and foul,
> By the smoky town in its murky cowl;
> Foul and dank, foul and dank,
> By wharf and sewer and slimy bank;

*Darker and darker the farther I go,*
*Baser and baser the richer I grow ;*
   *Who dare sport with the sin-defiled ?*
   *Shrink from me, turn from me, mother and child.*

   *Strong and free, strong and free,*
  *The floodgates are open, away to the sea,*
   *Free and strong, free and strong,*
  *Cleansing my streams as I hurry along,*
*To the golden sands, and the leaping bar,*
*And the taintless tide that awaits me afar.*
*As I lose myself in the infinite main,*
*Like a soul that has sinned and is pardoned again.*
   *Undefiled, for the undefiled ;*
   *Play by me, bathe in me, mother and child.*

So Tom went down ; and all the while he never saw the Irishwoman going down behind him.

"And is there care in heaven? and is there love
In heavenly spirits to these creatures base
That may compassion of their evils move?
There is :—else much more wretched were the case
Of men than beasts :   But oh ! the exceeding grace
Of Highest God that loves His creatures so,
And all His works with mercy doth embrace,
That blessed Angels He sends to and fro,
To serve to wicked man, to serve His wicked foe ! "

SPENSER.

# CHAPTER II

A MILE off, and a thousand feet down.

So Tom found it; though it seemed as if he could have chucked a pebble on to the back of the woman in the red petticoat who was weeding in the garden, or even across the dale to the rocks beyond. For the bottom of the valley was just one field broad, and on the other side ran the stream; and above it, grey crag, grey down, grey stair, grey moor walled up to heaven.

A quiet, silent, rich, happy place; a narrow crack cut deep into the earth; so deep, and so out of the way, that the bad bogies can hardly find it out. The name of the place is Vendale; and if you want to see it for yourself, you must go up into the High Craven, and search from Bolland Forest north by Ingleborough, to the Nine Standards and Cross Fell; and if you have not found it, you must turn south, and search the Lake Mountains, down to Scaw Fell and the sea; and then, if you have not found it, you must go northward again by merry Carlisle, and search the Cheviots all across, from Annan Water to Berwick Law; and then, whether you have found Vendale or not, you will have found such a country, and such a people, as ought to make you proud of being a British boy.

So Tom went to go down; and first he went down three hundred feet of steep heather, mixed up with loose brown gritstone, as rough as a file; which was not pleasant to his poor little heels, as he came bump, stump, jump, down the steep. And still he thought he could throw a stone into the garden.

Then he went down three hundred feet of limestone terraces, one below the other, as straight as if a carpenter had ruled them with his ruler and then cut them out with his chisel. There was no heath there, but—

First, a little grass slope, covered with the prettiest flowers, rockrose and saxifrage, and thyme and basil, and all sorts of sweet herbs.

Then bump down a two-foot step of limestone.

Then another bit of grass and flowers.

Then bump down a one-foot step.

Then another bit of grass and flowers for fifty yards, as steep as the house-roof, where he had to slide down on his dear little tail.

Then another step of stone, ten feet high; and there he had to stop himself, and crawl along the edge to find a crack; for if he had rolled over, he would have rolled right into the old woman's garden, and frightened her out of her wits.

Then, when he had found a dark narrow crack, full of green-stalked fern, such as hangs in the basket in the drawing-room, and had crawled down through it, with knees and elbows, as he would down a chimney, there was another grass slope, and another step, and so on, till—oh, dear me ! I wish it was all over; and so did he. And yet he thought he could throw a stone into the old woman's garden.

At last he came to a bank of beautiful shrubs ; white-beam with its great silver-backed leaves, and mountain-ash, and oak; and below them cliff and crag, cliff and crag, with great beds of crown-ferns and wood-sedge ; while through the shrubs he could see the stream sparkling, and hear it murmur on the white pebbles. He did not know that it was three hundred feet below.

You would have been giddy, perhaps, at looking down: but Tom was not. He was a brave little chimney-sweep ; and when he found himself on the top of a high cliff, instead of sitting down and cry- ing for his baba (though he never had had any baba to cry for), he said, "Ah, this will just suit me !" though he was very tired; and down he went, by stock and stone, sedge and ledge, bush and rush, as if he had been born a jolly little black ape, with four hands instead of two.

And all the while he never saw the Irishwoman coming down behind him.

But he was getting terribly tired now. The burning sun on the fells had sucked him up ; but the damp heat of the woody crag sucked him up still more ; and the perspiration ran out of the ends of his fingers and toes, and washed him cleaner than he had been for a whole year. But, of course, he dirtied everything terribly as he went. There has been a great black smudge all down the crag ever since. And there have been more black beetles in Vendale since than ever were known before; all, of course, owing to Tom's having blacked the original papa of them all, just as he was setting off to be married, with a sky-blue coat and scarlet leggings, as smart as a gardener's dog with a polyanthus in his mouth.

At last he got to the bottom. But, behold, it was not the bottom—as people usually find when they are coming down a mountain. For at the foot of the crag were heaps and heaps of fallen limestone of every size from that of your head to that of a stage-waggon, with holes between them full of sweet heath-fern; and before Tom got through them, he was out in the bright sunshine again; and then he felt, once for all and suddenly, as people generally do, that he was b-e-a-t, beat.

You must expect to be beat a few times in your life, little man, if you live such a life as a man ought to live, let you be as strong and healthy as you may: and when you are, you will find it a very ugly feeling. I hope that that day you may have a stout staunch friend by you who is not beat; for, if you have not, you had best lie where you are, and wait for better times, as poor Tom did.

He could not get on. The sun was burning, and yet he felt chill all over. He was quite empty, and yet he felt quite sick. There was but two hundred yards of smooth pasture between him and the cottage, and yet he could not walk down it. He could hear the stream murmuring only one field beyond it, and yet it seemed to him as if it was a hundred miles off.

He lay down on the grass till the beetles ran over him, and the flies settled on his nose. I don't know when he would have got up again, if the gnats and the midges had not taken compassion on him. But the gnats blew their trumpets so loud in his ear, and the midges nibbled so at his hands and face wherever they could find a place free from soot, that at last he woke up, and stumbled away, down over a low wall, and into a narrow road, and up to the cottage door.

And a neat pretty cottage it was, with clipped yew hedges all round the garden, and yews inside too, cut into peacocks and trumpets and teapots and all kinds of queer shapes. And out of the open door came a noise like that of the frogs on the Great-A, when they know that it is going to be scorching hot to-morrow—and how they know that I don't know, and you don't know, and nobody knows.

He came slowly up to the open door, which was all hung round with clematis and roses; and then peeped in, half afraid.

And there sat by the empty fireplace, which was filled with a pot of sweet herbs, the nicest old woman that ever was seen, in her red petticoat, and short dimity bedgown, and clean white cap, with a black silk handkerchief over it, tied under her chin. At her feet sat the grandfather of all the cats; and opposite her sat, on two benches, twelve or fourteen neat, rosy, chubby little children, learning their

Chris-cross-row; and gabble enough they made about it.

Such a pleasant cottage it was, with a shiny clean stone floor, and curious old prints on the walls, and an old black oak sideboard full of bright pewter and brass dishes, and a cuckoo clock in the corner, which began shouting as soon as Tom appeared: not that it was frightened at Tom, but that it was just eleven o'clock.

All the children started at Tom's dirty black figure,—the girls began to cry, and the boys began to laugh, and all pointed at him rudely enough; but Tom was too tired to care for that.

"What art thou, and what dost want?" cried the old dame. "A chimney-sweep! Away with thee! I'll have no sweeps here."

"Water," said poor little Tom, quite faint.

"Water? There's plenty i' the beck," she said, quite sharply.

"But I can't get there; I'm most clemmed with hunger and drought." And Tom sank down upon the door-step, and laid his head against the post.

And the old dame looked at him through her spectacles one minute, and two, and three; and then she said, "He's sick; and a bairn's a bairn, sweep or none."

"Water," said Tom.

"God forgive me!" and she put by her spectacles, and rose, and came to Tom. "Water's bad for thee; I'll give thee milk." And she toddled off into the next room, and brought a cup of milk and a bit of bread.

Tom drank the milk off at one draught, and then looked up, revived.

"Where didst come from?" said the dame.

"Over Fell, there," said Tom, and pointed up into the sky.

"Over Harthover? and down Lewthwaite Crag? Art sure thou art not lying?"

"Why should I?" said Tom, and leant his head against the post.

"And how got ye up there?"

"I came over from the Place"; and Tom was so tired and desperate he had no heart or time to think of a story, so he told all the truth in a few words.

"Bless thy little heart! And thou hast not been stealing, then?"

"No."

"Bless thy little heart! and I'll warrant not. Why, God's guided the bairn, because he was innocent! Away from the Place, and over Harthover Fell, and down Lewthwaite Crag! Who ever heard the like, if God hadn't led him? Why dost not eat thy bread?"

"I can't."

"It's good enough, for I made it myself."

"I can't," said Tom, and he laid his head on his knees, and then asked—

"Is it Sunday?"

"No, then; why should it be?"

"Because I hear the church-bells ringing so."

"Bless thy pretty heart! The bairn's sick. Come wi' me, and I'll hap thee up somewhere.

41

If thou wert a bit cleaner I'd put thee in my own bed, for the Lord's sake.   But come along here."

But when Tom tried to get up, he was so tired and giddy that she had to help him and lead him.

She put him in an outhouse upon soft sweet hay and an old rug, and bade him sleep off his walk, and she would come to him when school was over, in an hour's time.

And so she went in again, expecting Tom to fall fast asleep at once.

But Tom did not fall asleep.

Instead of it he turned and tossed and kicked about in the strangest way, and felt so hot all over that he longed to get into the river and cool himself; and then he fell half asleep, and dreamt that he heard the little white lady crying to him, "Oh, you're so dirty; go and be washed"; and then that he heard the Irishwoman saying, "Those that wish to be clean, clean they will be."   And then he heard the church-bells ring so loud, close to him too, that he was sure it must be Sunday, in spite of what the old dame had said; and he would go to church, and see what a church was like inside, for he had never been in one, poor little fellow, in all his life.   But the people would never let him come in, all over soot and dirt like that.   He must go to the river and wash first. And he said out loud again and again, though being half asleep he did not know it, "I must be clean, I must be clean."

And all of a sudden he found himself, not in the outhouse on the hay, but in the middle of a meadow, over the road, with the stream just before him, saying continually, " I must be clean, I must be clean." He had got there on his own legs, between sleep and awake, as children will often get out of bed, and go about the room, when they are not quite well. But he was not a bit surprised, and went on to the bank of the brook, and lay down on the grass, and looked into the clear, clear limestone water, with every pebble at the bottom bright and clean, while the little silver trout dashed about in fright at the sight of his black face; and he dipped his hand in and found it so cool, cool, cool; and he said, " I will be a fish; I will swim in the water; I must be clean, I must be clean."

So he pulled off all his clothes in such haste that he tore some of them, which was easy enough with such ragged old things. And he put his poor hot sore feet into the water; and then his legs ; and the farther he went in, the more the church-bells rang in his head.

" Ah," said Tom, " I must be quick and wash myself ; the bells are ringing quite loud now; and they will stop soon, and then the door will be shut, and I shall never be able to get in at all."

Tom was mistaken : for in England the church doors are left open all service time, for everybody who likes to come in, Churchman or Dissenter ; ay, even if he were a Turk or a Heathen ; and if any man dared to turn him out, as long as he behaved quietly, the good old English law would punish that man, as he deserved, for ordering any peaceable person out of God's house, which belongs

43

to all alike. But Tom did not know that, any more than he knew a great deal more which people ought to know.

And all the while he never saw the Irishwoman, not behind him this time, but before.

For just before he came to the river side, she had stept down into the cool clear water; and her shawl and her petticoat floated off her, and the green water-weeds floated round her sides, and the white water-lilies floated round her head, and the fairies of the stream came up from the bottom and bore her away and down upon their arms ; for she was the Queen of them all; and perhaps of more besides.

" Where have you been ? " they asked her.

" I have been smoothing sick folks' pillows, and whispering sweet dreams into their ears ; opening cottage casements, to let out the stifling air; coaxing little children away from gutters, and foul pools where fever breeds ; turning women from the gin-shop door, and staying men's hands as they were going to strike their wives ; doing all I can to help those who will not help themselves; and little enough that is, and weary work for me. But I have brought you a new little brother, and watched him safe all the way here."

Then all the fairies laughed for joy at the thought that they had a little brother coming.

" But mind, maidens, he must not see you, or know that you are here. He is but a savage now, and like the beasts which perish; and from the beasts which perish he must learn. So you must not play with him, or speak to him, or let him see you: but only keep him from being harmed."

Then the fairies were sad, because they could not play with their new brother, but they always did what they were told.

And their Queen floated away down the river; and whither she went, thither she came. But all this Tom, of course, never saw or heard: and perhaps if he had it would have made little difference in the story; for he was so hot and thirsty, and longed so to be clean for once, that he tumbled himself as quick as he could into the clear cool stream.

And he had not been in it two minutes before he fell fast asleep, into the quietest, sunniest, cosiest sleep that ever he had in his life; and he dreamt about the green meadows by which he had walked that morning, and the tall elm-trees, and the sleeping cows ; and after that he dreamt of nothing at all.

The reason of his falling into such a delightful sleep is very simple; and yet hardly any one has found it out. It was merely that the fairies took him.

Some people think that there are no fairies. Cousin Cramchild tells little folks so in his Conversations. Well, perhaps there are none—in Boston, U.S., where he was raised. There are only a clumsy lot of spirits there, who can't make people hear without thumping on the table : but they get their living thereby, and I suppose that is all they want. And Aunt Agitate, in her Arguments on political economy, says there are none.

Well, perhaps there are none—in her political economy. But it is a wide world, my little man —and thank Heaven for it, for else, between crinolines and theories, some of us would get squashed—and plenty of room in it for fairies, without people seeing them ; unless, of course, they look in the right place. The most wonderful and the strongest things in the world, you know, are just the things which no one can see. There is life in you ; and it is the life in you which makes you grow, and move, and think : and yet you can't see it. And there is steam in a steam-engine ; and that is what makes it move : and yet you can't see it ; and so there may be fairies in the world, and they may be just what makes the world go round to the old tune of

> " *C'est l'amour, l'amour, l'amour*
> *Qui fait le monde à la ronde :* "

and yet no one may be able to see them except those whose hearts are going round to that same tune. At all events, we will make believe that there are fairies in the world. It will not be the last time by many a one that we shall have to make believe. And yet, after all, there is no need for that. There must be fairies ; for this is a fairy tale : and how can one have a fairy tale if there are no fairies ?

You don't see the logic of that ? Perhaps not. Then please not to see the logic of a great many arguments exactly like it, which you will hear before your beard is grey.

The kind old dame came back at twelve, when school was over, to look at Tom: but there was no Tom there. She looked about for his footprints; but the ground was so hard that there was no slot, as they say in dear old North Devon. And if you grow up to be a brave healthy man, you may know some day what no slot means, and know too, I hope, what a slot does mean—a broad slot, with blunt claws, which makes a man put out his cigar, and set his teeth, and tighten his girths, when he sees it; and what his rights mean, if he has them, brow, bay, tray, and points; and see something worth seeing between Haddon Wood and Countisbury Cliff, with good Mr. Palk Collyns to show you the way, and mend your bones as fast as you smash them. Only when that jolly day comes, please don't break your neck; stogged in a mire you never will be, I trust; for you are a heath-cropper bred and born.

So the old dame went in again quite sulky, thinking that little Tom had tricked her with a false story, and shammed ill, and then run away again.

But she altered her mind the next day. For, when Sir John and the rest of them had run themselves out of breath, and lost Tom, they went back again, looking very foolish.

And they looked more foolish still when Sir John heard more of the story from the nurse; and more foolish still, again, when they heard the whole story from Miss Ellie, the little lady in white. All she had seen was a poor little black chimney-sweep, crying and sobbing, and going to get up the chimney again. Of course, she was very much frightened: and no wonder. But that was all. The boy had taken nothing in the room; by the mark of his little sooty feet, they could see that he had never been off the hearthrug till the nurse caught hold of him. It was all a mistake.

So Sir John told Grimes to go home, and promised him five shillings if he would bring the boy quietly up to him, without beating him, that he might be sure of the truth. For he took for granted, and Grimes too, that Tom had made his way home.

But no Tom came back to Mr. Grimes that evening; and he went to the police-office, to tell them to look out for the boy. But no Tom was heard of. As for his having gone over those great fells to Vendale, they no more dreamed of that than of his having gone to the moon.

So Mr. Grimes came up to Harthover next day with a very sour face; but when he got there, Sir John was over the hills and far away; and Mr. Grimes had to sit in the outer servants' hall all day, and drink strong ale to wash away his sorrows; and they were washed away long before Sir John came back.

For good Sir John had slept very badly that night; and he said to his lady, "My dear, the boy must have got over into the grouse-moors, and lost himself; and he lies very heavily on my conscience, poor little lad. But I know what I will do."

So, at five the next morning up he got, and into his bath, and into his shooting-jacket and gaiters, and into the stableyard, like a fine old English gentleman, with a face as red as a rose, and a hand as hard as a table, and a back as broad as a bullock's; and bade them bring his shooting pony, and the keeper to come on his pony, and the huntsman, and the first whip, and the second whip, and the under-keeper with the bloodhound in a leash—a great dog as tall as a calf, of the colour of a gravel-walk, with mahogany ears and nose, and a throat like a church-bell.  They took him up to the place where Tom had gone into the wood; and there the hound lifted up his mighty voice, and told them all he knew.

Then he took them to the place where Tom had climbed the wall; and they shoved it down, and all got through.

And then the wise dog took them over the moor, and over the fells, step by step, very slowly; for the scent was a day old, you know, and very light from the heat and drought.  But that was why cunning old Sir John started at five in the morning.

And at last he came to the top of Lewthwaite Crag, and there he bayed, and looked up in their faces, as much as to say, " I tell you he is gone down here ! "

They could hardly believe that Tom would have gone so far; and when they looked at that awful cliff, they could never believe that he would have dared to face it.  But if the dog said so, it must be true.

49

"Heaven forgive us!" said Sir John. "If we find him at all, we shall find him lying at the bottom." And he slapped his great hand upon his great thigh, and said—

"Who will go down over Lewthwaite Crag, and see if that boy is alive? Oh that I were twenty years younger, and I would go down myself!" And so he would have done, as well as any sweep in the county. Then he said—

"Twenty pounds to the man who brings me that boy alive!" and as was his way, what he said he meant.

Now among the lot was a little groom-boy, a very little groom indeed; and he was the same who had ridden up the court, and told Tom to come to the Hall; and he said—

"Twenty pounds or none, I will go down over Lewthwaite Crag, if it's only for the poor boy's sake. For he was as civil a spoken little chap as ever climbed a flue."

So down over Lewthwaite Crag he went: a very smart groom he was at the top, and a very shabby one at the bottom; for he tore his gaiters, and he tore his breeches, and he tore his jacket, and he burst his braces, and he burst his boots, and he lost his hat, and what was worst of all, he lost his shirt pin, which he prized very much, for it was gold, and he had won it in a raffle at Malton, and there was a figure at the top of it, of t'ould mare, noble old Beeswing herself, as natural as life; so it was a really severe loss: but he never saw anything of Tom.

And all the while Sir John and the rest were riding round, full three miles to the right, and back again, to get into Vendale, and to the foot of the crag.

When they came to the old dame's school, all the children came out to see. And the old dame came out too; and when she saw Sir John, she curtsied very low, for she was a tenant of his.

"Well, dame, and how are you?" said Sir John.

"Blessings on you as broad as your back, Harthover," says she—she didn't call him Sir John, but only Harthover, for that is the fashion in the North country—"and welcome into Vendale: but you're no hunting the fox this time of the year?"

"I am hunting, and strange game too," said he.

"Blessings on your heart, and what makes you look so sad the morn?"

"I'm looking for a lost child, a chimney-sweep, that is run away."

"Oh, Harthover, Harthover," says she, "ye were always a just man and a merciful; and ye'll no harm the poor little lad if I give you tidings of him?"

"Not I, not I, dame. I'm afraid we hunted him out of the house all on a miserable mistake, and the hound has brought him to the top of Lewthwaite Crag, and——"

Whereat the old dame broke out crying, without letting him finish his story.

"So he told me the truth after all, poor little

dear ! Ah, first thoughts are best, and a body's heart'll guide them right, if they will but hearken to it." And then she told Sir John all.

"Bring the dog here, and lay him on," said Sir John, without another word, and he set his teeth very hard.

And the dog opened at once; and went away at the back of the cottage, over the road, and over the meadow, and through a bit of alder copse; and there, upon an alder stump, they saw Tom's clothes lying. And then they knew as much about it all as there was any need to know.

And Tom ?

Ah, now comes the most wonderful part of this wonderful story. Tom, when he woke, for of course he woke—children always wake after they have slept exactly as long as is good for them— found himself swimming about in the stream, being about four inches, or—that I may be accurate—$3·87902$ inches long, and having round the parotid region of his fauces a set of external gills (I hope you understand all the big words) just like those of a sucking eft, which he mistook for a lace frill, till he pulled at them, found he hurt himself, and made up his mind that they were part of himself, and best left alone.

In fact, the fairies had turned him into a water-baby.

A water-baby ? You never heard of a water-baby. Perhaps not. That is the very reason why this story was written. There are a great many things in the world which you never heard of;

and a great many more which nobody ever heard of; and a great many things, too, which nobody will ever hear of, at least until the coming of the Cocqcigrues, when man shall be the measure of all things.

"But there are no such things as water-babies."

How do you know that? Have you been there to see? And if you had been there to see, and had seen none, that would not prove that there were none. If Mr. Garth does not find a fox in Eversley Wood—as folks sometimes fear he never will—that does not prove that there are no such things as foxes. And as is Eversley Wood to all the woods in England, so are the waters we know to all the waters in the world. And no one has a right to say that no water-babies exist, till they have seen no water-babies existing; which is quite a different thing, mind, from not seeing water-babies; and a thing which nobody ever did, or perhaps ever will do.

"But surely if there were water-babies, some-body would have caught one at least?"

Well. How do you know that somebody has not?

"But they would have put it into spirits, or into the *Illustrated News*, or perhaps cut it into two halves, poor dear little thing, and sent one to Professor Owen, and one to Professor Huxley, to see what they would each say about it."

Ah, my dear little man! that does not follow at all, as you will see before the end of the story.

"But a water-baby is contrary to nature."

Well, but, my dear little man, you must learn to talk about such things, when you grow older, in a very different way from that. You must not talk about "ain't" and "can't" when you speak of this great wonderful world round you, of which the wisest man knows only the very smallest corner, and is, as the great Sir Isaac Newton said, only a child picking up pebbles on the shore of a boundless ocean.

You must not say that this cannot be, or that that is contrary to nature. You do not know what Nature is, or what she can do; and nobody knows; not even Sir Roderick Murchison, or Professor Owen, or Professor Sedgwick, or Professor Huxley, or Mr. Darwin, or Professor Faraday, or Mr. Grove, or any other of the great men whom good boys are taught to respect. They are very wise men; and you must listen respectfully to all they say: but even if they should say, which I am sure they never would, "That cannot exist. That is contrary to nature," you must wait a little, and see; for perhaps even they may be wrong. It is only children who read Aunt Agitate's Arguments, or Cousin Cramchild's Conversations; or lads who go to popular lectures, and see a man pointing at a few big ugly pictures on the wall, or making nasty smells with bottles and squirts, for an hour or two, and calling that anatomy or chemistry—who talk about "cannot exist," and "contrary to nature." Wise men are afraid to say that there is anything contrary to nature, except what is contrary to mathematical truth; for two and two cannot make five, and two straight lines cannot join twice, and a part cannot be as great as the whole, and so on (at least, so it seems at present): but the wiser men are, the less they talk about "cannot." That is a very rash, dangerous word, that "cannot"; and if people use it too often, the Queen of all the Fairies, who makes the clouds thunder and the fleas bite, and takes just as much trouble about one as about the other, is apt to astonish them suddenly by showing them, that though they say she cannot, yet she can, and what is more, will, whether they approve or not.

And therefore it is, that there are dozens and hundreds of things in the world which we should certainly have said were contrary to nature, if we did not see them going on under our eyes all day long. If people had never seen little seeds grow into great plants and trees, of quite different shape from themselves, and these trees again produce fresh seeds, to grow into fresh trees, they would have said, "The thing cannot be; it is contrary to nature." And they would have been quite as right in saying so, as in saying that most other things cannot be.

Or suppose again, that you had come, like M. Du Chaillu, a traveller from unknown parts; and that no human being had ever seen or heard of an elephant. And suppose that you described him to people, and said, "This is the shape, and plan, and anatomy of the beast, and of his feet, and of his trunk, and of his grinders, and of his tusks, though they are not tusks at all, but two fore teeth run mad; and this is the section of his skull, more like a mushroom than a reasonable skull of a reasonable or unreasonable beast; and so forth, and so forth; and though the beast (which I assure you I have seen and shot) is first cousin to the little hairy coney of Scripture, second cousin to a pig, and (I suspect) thirteenth or fourteenth cousin to a rabbit, yet he is the wisest of all beasts, and can do everything save read, write, and cast accounts." People would surely have said, "Nonsense; your elephant is contrary to nature"; and have thought you were telling stories—as the French thought of Le Vaillant when he came back to Paris and said that he had shot a giraffe; and as the king of the Cannibal Islands thought of the English sailor, when he said that in his country water turned to marble, and rain fell as feathers. They would tell you, the more they knew of science, "Your elephant is an impossible monster, contrary to the laws of comparative anatomy, as far as yet known." To which you would answer the less, the more you thought.

Did not learned men, too, hold, till within the last twenty-five years, that a flying dragon was an impossible monster? And do we not now know that there are hundreds of them found fossil up and down the world? People call them Pterodactyles: but that is only because they are ashamed to call them flying dragons, after denying so long that flying dragons could exist.

The truth is, that folks' fancy that such and

such things cannot be, simply because they have not seen them, is worth no more than a savage's fancy that there cannot be such a thing as a locomotive, because he never saw one running wild in the forest.  Wise men know that their business is to examine what is, and not to settle what is not.  They know that there are elephants; they know that there have been flying dragons ; and the wiser they are, the less inclined they will be to say positively that there are no water-babies.

No water-babies, indeed ?  Why, wise men of old said that everything on earth had its double in the water; and you may see that that is, if not quite true, still quite as true as most other theories which you are likely to hear for many a day.  There are land-babies—then why not water-babies ?  *Are there not water-rats, water-flies, water-crickets, water-crabs, water-tortoises, water-scorpions, water-tigers and water-hogs, water-cats and water-dogs, sea-lions and sea-bears, sea-horses and sea-elephants, sea-mice and sea-urchins, sea-razors and sea-pens, sea-combs and sea-fans; and of plants, are there not water-grass, and water-crowfoot, water-milfoil, and so on, without end ?*

"But all these things are only nicknames; the water things are not really akin to the land things."

That's not always true.  They are, in millions of cases, not only of the same family, but actually the same individual creatures.  Do not even you know that a green drake, and an alder-fly, and a dragon-fly, live under water till they change their skins, just as Tom changed his ?  And if a water animal can continually change into a land animal, why should not a land animal sometimes change into a water animal ?   Don't be put down by any of Cousin Cramchild's arguments, but stand up to him like a man, and answer him (quite respectfully, of course) thus:—

If Cousin Cramchild says, that if there are water-babies, they must grow into water-men, ask him how he knows that they do not ? and then, how he knows that they must, any more than the Proteus of the Adelsberg caverns grows into a perfect newt.

If he says that it is too strange a transformation for a land-baby to turn into a water-baby, ask him if he ever heard of the transformation of Syllis, or the Distomas, or the common jelly-fish, of which M. Quatrefages says excellently well —" Who would not exclaim that a miracle had come to pass, if he saw a reptile come out of the egg dropped by the hen in his poultry-yard, and the reptile give birth at once to an indefinite number of fishes and birds ?   Yet the history of the jelly-fish is quite as wonderful as that would be." Ask him if he knows about all this; and if he does not, tell him to go and look for himself ; and advise him (very respectfully, of course) to settle no more what strange things cannot happen, till he has seen what strange things do happen every day.

If he says that things cannot degrade, that is, change downwards into lower forms, ask him, who told him that water-babies were lower than land-babies ?   But even if they were, does he know about the strange degradation of the common goose-barnacles, which one finds sticking on ships' bottoms; or the still stranger degradation of some cousins of theirs, of which one hardly likes to talk, so shocking and ugly it is?

And, lastly, if he says (as he most certainly will) that these transformations only take place in the lower animals, and not in the higher, say that that seems to little boys, and to some grown people, a very strange fancy. For if the changes of the lower animals are so wonderful, and so difficult to discover, why should not there be changes in the higher animals far more wonderful, and far more difficult to discover? And may not man, the crown and flower of all things, undergo some change as much more wonderful than all the rest, as the Great Exhibition is more wonderful than a rabbit-burrow? Let him answer that. And if he says (as he will) that not having seen such a change in his experience, he is not bound to believe it, ask him respectfully, where his microscope has been? Does not each of us, in coming into this world, go through a transformation just as wonderful as that of a sea-egg, or a butterfly? and do not reason and analogy, as well as Scripture, tell us that that transformation is not the last? and that, though what we shall be, we know not, yet we are here but as the crawling caterpillar, and shall be hereafter as the perfect fly. The old Greeks, heathens as they were, saw as much as that two thousand years ago; and I care very little for Cousin Cramchild, if he sees even less than they. And so forth, and so forth, till he is quite cross. And then tell him that if there are no water-babies, at least there ought to be ; and that, at least, he cannot answer.

And meanwhile, my dear little man, till you know a great deal more about nature than Professor Owen and Professor Huxley put together, don't tell me about what cannot be, or fancy that anything is too wonderful to be true. "We are fearfully and wonderfully made," said old David ; and so we are ; and so is everything around us, down to the very deal table. Yes ; much more fearfully and wonderfully made, already, is the table, as it stands now, nothing but a piece of dead deal wood, than if, as foxes say, and geese believe, spirits could make it dance, or talk to you by rapping on it.

Am I in earnest ? Oh dear no ! Don't you know that this is a fairy tale, and all fun and pretence; and that you are not to believe one word of it, even if it is true?

But at all events, so it happened to Tom. And, therefore, the keeper, and the groom, and Sir John made a great mistake, and were very unhappy (Sir John at least) without any reason, when they found a black thing in the water, and said it was Tom's body, and that he had been drowned. They were utterly mistaken. Tom was quite alive; and cleaner, and merrier, than he ever had been. The fairies had washed him, you see, in the swift river, so thoroughly, that not only his dirt, but his whole husk and shell had been washed quite off him, and the pretty little real Tom was washed out of the inside of it, and swam away, as a caddis does when its case of stones and silk is bored through, and away it goes on its back, paddling to the shore, there to split its skin, and fly away as a caperer, on four fawn-coloured wings, with long legs and horns. They are foolish fellows, the caperers, and fly into the candle at night, if you leave the door open. We will hope Tom will be wiser, now he has got safe out of his sooty old shell.

But good Sir John did not understand all this, not being a fellow of the Linnæan Society; and he took it into his head that Tom was drowned. When they looked into the empty pockets of his shell, and found no jewels there, nor money— nothing but three marbles, and a brass button with a string to it—then Sir John did something as like crying as ever he did in his life, and blamed himself more bitterly than he need have done. So he cried, and the groom-boy cried, and the huntsman cried, and the dame cried, and the little girl cried, and the dairymaid cried, and the old nurse cried (for it was somewhat her fault), and my lady cried, for though people have wigs, that is no reason why they should not have hearts; but the keeper did not cry, though he had been so good-natured to Tom the morning before; for he was so dried up with running after poachers, that you could no more get tears out of him than milk out of leather: and Grimes did not cry, for Sir John gave him ten pounds, and he drank it all in a week. Sir John sent, far and wide, to find Tom's father and mother: but he might have looked till Doomsday for them, for one was dead, and the other was in Botany Bay. And the little girl would not play with her dolls for

Those are the words : but they are only the body of it : the soul of the song was the dear old woman's sweet face, and sweet voice, and the sweet old air to which she sang ; and that, alas ! one cannot put on paper. And at last she grew so stiff and lame, that the angels were forced to carry her ; and they helped her on with her wedding-dress, and carried her up over Harthover Fells, and a long way beyond that too ; and there was a new schoolmistress in Vendale, and we will hope that she was not certificated.

And all the while Tom was swimming about in the river, with a pretty little lace-collar of gills about his neck, as lively as a grig, and as clean as a fresh-run salmon.

Now if you don't like my story, then go to the schoolroom and learn your multiplication-table, and see if you like that better. Some people, no doubt, would do so. So much the better for us, if not for them. It takes all sorts, they say, to make a world.

# CHAPTER III

Tom was now quite amphibious. You do not know what that means ?

You had better, then, ask the nearest Government pupil-teacher, who may possibly answer you smartly enough, thus—

"Amphibious. Adjective, derived from two Greek words, *amphï*, a fish, and *bios*, a beast. An animal supposed by our ignorant ancestors to be compounded of a fish and a beast; which therefore, like the hippopotamus, can't live on the land, and dies in the water."

However that may be, Tom was amphibious: and what is better still, he was clean. For the first time in his life, he felt how comfortable it was to have nothing on him but himself. But he only enjoyed it: he did not know it, or think about it; just as you enjoy life and health, and yet never think about being alive and healthy; and may it be long before you have to think about it !

He did not remember having ever been dirty. Indeed, he did not remember any of his old troubles, being tired, or hungry, or beaten, or sent up dark chimneys. Since that sweet sleep, he had forgotten all about his master, and Harthover

Place, and the little white girl, and in a word, all that had happened to him when he lived before; and what was best of all, he had forgotten all the bad words which he had learned from Grimes, and the rude boys with whom he used to play.

That is not strange: for you know, when you came into this world, and became a land-baby, you remembered nothing. So why should he, when he became a water-baby?

Then have you lived before?

My dear child, who can tell? One can only tell that, by remembering something which happened where we lived before; and as we remember nothing, we know nothing about it; and no book, and no man, can ever tell us certainly.

There was a wise man once, a very wise man, and a very good man, who wrote a poem about the feelings which some children have about having lived before; and this is what he said—

> " *Our birth is but a sleep and a forgetting;*
> *The soul that rises with us, our life's star,*
> *Hath elsewhere had its setting,*
> *And cometh from afar:*
> *Not in entire forgetfulness,*
> *And not in utter nakedness,*
> *But trailing clouds of glory, do we come*
> *From God, who is our home.*"

There, you can know no more than that. But if I was you, I would believe that. For then the great fairy Science, who is likely to be queen of

all the fairies for many a year to come, can only
do you good, and never do you harm ; and instead
of fancying, with some people, that your body
makes your soul, as if a steam-engine could make
its own coke ; or, with some people, that your
soul has nothing to do with your body, but is only
stuck into it like a pin into a pin-cushion, to fall
out with the first shake ;—you will believe the
one true,

| | |
|---|---|
| *orthodox*, | *inductive*, |
| *rational*, | *deductive*, |
| *philosophical*, | *seductive*, |
| *logical*, | *productive*, |
| *irrefragable*, | *salutary*, |
| *nominalistic*, | *comfortable*, |
| *realistic*, | |
| *and on-all-accounts-to-be-received* | |

doctrine of this wonderful fairy tale ; which is,
that your soul makes your body, just as a snail
makes his shell.   For the rest, it is enough for us
to be sure that whether or not we lived before, we
shall live again ; though not, I hope, as poor little
heathen Tom did.   For he went downward into
the water : but we, I hope, shall go upward to a
very different place.

But Tom was very happy in the water.   He
had been sadly overworked in the land-world ; and
so now, to make up for that, he had nothing but
holidays in the water-world for a long, long time
to come.   He had nothing to do now but enjoy
himself, and look at all the pretty things which are

to be seen in the cool clear water-world, where the sun is never too hot, and the frost is never too cold.

And what did he live on? Water-cresses, per-haps; or perhaps water-gruel, and water-milk; too many land-babies do so likewise. But we do not know what one-tenth of the water-things eat; so we are not answerable for the water-babies.

Sometimes he went along the smooth gravel water-ways, looking at the crickets which ran in and out among the stones, as rabbits do on land; or he climbed over the ledges of rock, and saw the sand-pipes hanging in thousands, with every one of them a pretty little head and legs peeping out; or he went into a still corner, and watched the caddises eating dead sticks as greedily as you would eat plum-pudding, and building their houses with silk and glue. Very fanciful ladies they were; none of them would keep to the same materials for a day. One would begin with some pebbles; then she would stick on a piece of green wood; then she found a shell, and stuck it on too; and the poor shell was alive, and did not like at all being taken to build houses with: but the caddis did not let him have any voice in the matter, being rude and selfish, as vain people are apt to be; then she stuck on a piece of rotten wood, then a very smart pink stone, and so on, till she was patched all over like an Irishman's coat. Then she found a long straw, five times as long as herself, and said, "Hurrah! my sister has a tail, and I'll have one too"; and she stuck it on her back, and marched about with it quite proud, though it was very inconvenient indeed.  And, at that, tails became all the fashion among the caddis-baits in that pool, as they were at the end of the Long Pond last May, and they all toddled about with long straws sticking out behind, getting between each other's legs, and tumbling over each other, and looking so ridiculous, that Tom laughed at them till he cried, as we did. But they were quite right, you know; for people must always follow the fashion, even if it be spoon-bonnets.

Then sometimes he came to a deep still reach; and there he saw the water-forests.  They would have looked to you only little weeds: but Tom, you must remember, was so little that everything looked a hundred times as big to him as it does to you, just as things do to a minnow, who sees and catches the little water-creatures which you can only see in a microscope.

And in the water-forest he saw the water-monkeys and water-squirrels (they had all six legs, though; everything almost has six legs in the water, except efts and water-babies); and nimbly enough they ran among the branches.  There were water-flowers there too, in thousands; and Tom tried to pick them: but as soon as he touched them, they drew themselves in and turned into knots of jelly; and then Tom saw that they were all alive—bells, and stars, and wheels, and flowers, of all beautiful shapes and colours; and all alive and busy, just as Tom was.  So now he found that there was a great deal more in the world than he had fancied at first sight.

There was one wonderful little fellow, too, who peeped out of the top of a house built of round bricks.   He had two big wheels, and one little one, all over teeth, spinning round and round like the wheels in a thrashing-machine; and Tom stood and stared at him, to see what he was going to make with his machinery.   And what do you think he was doing ?   Brick-making.   With his two big wheels he swept together all the mud which floated in the water : all that was nice in it he put into his stomach and ate ; and all the mud he put into the little wheel on his breast, which really was a round hole set with teeth ; and there he spun it into a neat hard round brick ; and then he took it and stuck it on the top of his house-wall, and set to work to make another.   Now was not he a clever little fellow ?

Tom thought so : but when he wanted to talk to him the brick-maker was much too busy and proud of his work to take notice of him.

Now you must know that all the things under the water talk ; only not such a language as ours ; but such as horses, and dogs, and cows, and birds talk to each other ; and Tom soon learned to understand them and talk to them ; so that he might have had very pleasant company if he had only been a good boy.   But I am sorry to say, he was too like some other little boys, very fond of hunting and tormenting creatures for mere sport.   Some people say that boys cannot help it ; that it is nature, and only a proof that we are all originally descended from beasts of prey.   But whether it is nature or not, little boys can help it, and must help it. For if they have naughty, low, mischievous tricks in their nature, as monkeys have, that is no reason why they should give way to those tricks like monkeys, who know no better. And therefore they must not torment dumb creatures; for if they do, a certain old lady who is coming will surely give them exactly what they deserve.

But Tom did not know that; and he pecked and howked the poor water-things about sadly, till they were all afraid of him, and got out of his way, or crept into their shells; so he had no one to speak to or play with.

The water-fairies, of course, were very sorry to see him so unhappy, and longed to take him, and tell him how naughty he was, and teach him to be good, and to play and romp with him too: but they had been forbidden to do that. Tom had to learn his lesson for himself by sound and sharp experience, as many another foolish person has to do, though there may be many a kind heart yearning over them all the while, and longing to teach them what they can only teach themselves.

At last one day he found a caddis, and wanted it to peep out of its house: but its house-door was shut. He had never seen a caddis with a house-door before: so what must he do, the meddlesome little fellow, but pull it open, to see what the poor lady was doing inside. What a shame! How should you like to have any one breaking your bedroom-door in, to see how you looked when you were in bed? So Tom broke to pieces the door, which was the prettiest little grating of silk, stuck all over with shining bits of crystal; and when he looked in, the caddis poked out her head, and it had turned into just the shape of a bird's. But when Tom spoke to her she could not answer; for her mouth and face were tight tied up in a new night-cap of neat pink skin. However, if she didn't answer, all the other caddises did; for they held up their hands and shrieked like the cats in Struwwelpeter: "*Oh, you nasty horrid boy; there you are at it again! And she had just laid herself up for a fortnight's sleep, and then she would have come out with such beautiful wings, and flown about, and laid such lots of eggs: and now you have broken her door, and she can't mend it because her mouth is tied up for a fortnight, and she will die. Who sent you here to worry us out of our lives?*"

So Tom swam away. He was very much ashamed of himself, and felt all the naughtier; as little boys do when they have done wrong and won't say so.

Then he came to a pool full of little trout, and began tormenting them, and trying to catch them: but they slipped through his fingers, and jumped clean out of water in their fright. But as Tom chased them, he came close to a great dark hover under an alder root, and out floushed a huge old brown trout ten times as big as he was, and ran right against him, and knocked all the breath out of his body; and I don't know which was the more frightened of the two.

Then he went on sulky and lonely, as he

deserved to be; and under a bank he saw a very ugly dirty creature sitting, about half as big as himself; which had six legs, and a big stomach, and a most ridiculous head with two great eyes and a face just like a donkey's.

"Oh," said Tom, "you are an ugly fellow to be sure!" and he began making faces at him; and put his nose close to him, and halloed at him, like a very rude boy.

When, hey presto; all the thing's donkey-face came off in a moment, and out popped a long arm with a pair of pincers at the end of it, and caught Tom by the nose. It did not hurt him much; but it held him quite tight.

"Yah, ah! Oh, let me go!" cried Tom.

"Then let me go," said the creature. "I want to be quiet. I want to split."

Tom promised to let him alone, and he let go. "Why do you want to split?" said Tom.

"Because my brothers and sisters have all split, and turned into beautiful creatures with wings; and I want to split too. Don't speak to me. I am sure I shall split. I will split!"

Tom stood still, and watched him. And he swelled himself, and puffed, and stretched himself out stiff, and at last—crack, puff, bang—he opened all down his back, and then up to the top of his head.

And out of his inside came the most slender, elegant, soft creature, as soft and smooth as Tom: but very pale and weak, like a little child who has been ill a long time in a dark room. It moved its legs very feebly; and looked about it half ashamed, like a girl when she goes for the first time into a ballroom ; and then it began walking slowly up a grass stem to the top of the water.

Tom was so astonished that he never said a word: but he stared with all his eyes. And he went up to the top of the water too, and peeped out to see what would happen.

And as the creature sat in the warm bright sun, a wonderful change came over it. It grew strong and firm ; the most lovely colours began to show on its body, blue and yellow and black, spots and bars and rings ; out of its back rose four great wings of bright brown gauze ; and its eyes grew so large that they filled all its head, and shone like ten thousand diamonds.

" Oh, you beautiful creature ! " said Tom ; and he put out his hand to catch it.

But the thing whirred up into the air, and hung poised on its wings a moment, and then settled down again by Tom quite fearless.

" No ! " it said, " you cannot catch me. I am a dragon-fly now, the king of all the flies ; and I shall dance in the sunshine, and hawk over the river, and catch gnats, and have a beautiful wife like myself. I know what I shall do. Hurrah ! " And he flew away into the air, and began catching gnats.

" Oh ! come back, come back," cried Tom, " you beautiful creature. I have no one to play with, and I am so lonely here. If you will but come back I will never try to catch you."

"I don't care whether you do or not," said the dragon-fly; "for you can't.  But when I have had my dinner, and looked a little about this pretty place, I will come back, and have a little chat about all I have seen in my travels.  Why, what a huge tree this is! and what huge leaves on it!"

It was only a big dock: but you know the dragon-fly had never seen any but little water-trees; starwort, and milfoil, and water-crowfoot, and such like; so it did look very big to him. Besides, he was very short-sighted, as all dragon-flies are; and never could see a yard before his nose; any more than a great many other folks, who are not half as handsome as he.

The dragon-fly did come back, and chatted away with Tom.  He was a little conceited about his fine colours and his large wings; but you know, he had been a poor dirty ugly creature all his life before; so there were great excuses for him.  He was very fond of talking about all the wonderful things he saw in the trees and the meadows; and Tom liked to listen to him, for he had forgotten all about them.  So in a little while they became great friends.

And I am very glad to say, that Tom learned such a lesson that day, that he did not torment creatures for a long time after.  And then the caddises grew quite tame, and used to tell him strange stories about the way they built their houses, and changed their skins, and turned at last into winged flies; till Tom began to long to change his skin, and have wings like them some day.

And the trout and he made it up (for trout very soon forget if they have been frightened and hurt). So Tom used to play with them at hare and hounds, and great fun they had; and he used to try to leap out of the water, head over heels, as they did before a shower came on; but somehow he never could manage it. He liked most, though, to see them rising at the flies, as they sailed round and round under the shadow of the great oak, where the beetles fell flop into the water, and the green caterpillars let themselves down from the boughs by silk ropes for no reason at all; and then changed their foolish minds for no reason at all either; and hauled themselves up again into the tree, rolling up the rope in a ball between their paws; which is a very clever rope-dancer's trick, and neither Blondin nor Leotard could do it: but why they should take so much trouble about it no one can tell; for they cannot get their living, as Blondin and Leotard do, by trying to break their necks on a string.

And very often Tom caught them just as they touched the water; and caught the alder-flies, and the caperers, and the cock-tailed duns and spinners, yellow, and brown, and claret, and grey, and gave them to his friends the trout. Perhaps he was not quite kind to the flies; but one must do a good turn to one's friends when one can.

And at last he gave up catching even the flies; for he made acquaintance with one by accident and found him a very merry little fellow. And this was the way it happened; and it is all quite true.

He was basking at the top of the water one hot day in July, catching duns and feeding the trout, when he saw a new sort, a dark grey little fellow with a brown head. He was a very little fellow indeed : but he made the most of himself, as people ought to do. He cocked up his head, and he cocked up his wings, and he cocked up his tail, and he cocked up the two whisks at his tail-end, and, in short, he looked the cockiest little man of all little men. And so he proved to be; for instead of getting away, he hopped upon Tom's finger, and sat there as bold as nine tailors; and he cried out in the tiniest, shrillest, squeakiest little voice you ever heard,

" Much obliged to you, indeed; but I don't want it yet."

" Want what?" said Tom, quite taken aback by his impudence.

" Your leg, which you are kind enough to hold out for me to sit on. I must just go and see after my wife for a few minutes. Dear me ! what a troublesome business a family is !" (though the idle little rogue did nothing at all, but left his poor wife to lay all the eggs by herself). " When I come back, I shall be glad of it, if you'll be so good as to keep it sticking out just so"; and off he flew.

Tom thought him a very cool sort of personage; and still more so, when, in five minutes he came back, and said—" Ah, you were tired waiting ? Well, your other leg will do as well."

And he popped himself down on Tom's knee, and began chatting away in his squeaking voice.

" So you live under the water ? It's a low place. I lived there for some time ; and was very shabby and dirty. But I didn't choose that that should last. So I turned respectable, and came up to the top, and put on this grey suit. It's a very business-like suit, you think, don't you ? "

" Very neat and quiet indeed," said Tom.

" Yes, one must be quiet and neat and respectable, and all that sort of thing for a little, when one becomes a family man. But I'm tired of it, that's the truth. I've done quite enough business, I consider, in the last week, to last me my life. So I shall put on a ball-dress, and go out and be a smart man, and see the gay world, and have a dance or two. Why shouldn't one be jolly if one can ? "

" And what will become of your wife ? "

" Oh ! she is a very plain stupid creature, and that's the truth ; and thinks about nothing but eggs. If she chooses to come, why she may; and if not, why I go without her ;—and here I go."

And, as he spoke, he turned quite pale, and then quite white.

" Why, you're ill ! " said Tom. But he did not answer.

" You're dead," said Tom, looking at him as he stood on his knee as white as a ghost.

"No, I ain't!" answered a little squeaking voice over his head. "This is me up here, in my ball-dress; and that's my skin. Ha, ha! you could not do such a trick as that!"

And no more Tom could, nor Houdin, nor Robin, nor Frikell, nor all the conjurers in the world. For the little rogue had jumped clean out of his own skin, and left it standing on Tom's knee, eyes, wings, legs, tail, exactly as if it had been alive.

"Ha, ha!" he said, and he jerked and skipped up and down, never stopping an instant, just as if he had St. Vitus's dance. "Ain't I a pretty fellow now?"

And so he was; for his body was white, and his tail orange, and his eyes all the colours of a peacock's tail. And what was the oddest of all, the whisks at the end of his tail had grown five times as long as they were before.

"Ah!" said he, "now I will see the gay world. My living won't cost me much, for I have no mouth, you see, and no inside; so I can never be hungry nor have the stomach-ache neither."

No more he had. He had grown as dry and hard and empty as a quill, as such silly shallow-hearted fellows deserve to grow.

But, instead of being ashamed of his emptiness, he was quite proud of it, as a good many fine gentlemen are, and began flirting and flipping up and down, and singing—

> " *My wife shall dance, and I shall sing,*
>    *So merrily pass the day;*
> *For I hold it for quite the wisest thing,*
>    *To drive dull care away.*"

And he danced up and down for three days and three nights, till he grew so tired, that he tumbled into the water, and floated down. But what became of him Tom never knew, and he himself never minded; for Tom heard him singing to the last, as he floated down—

> " *To drive dull care away-ay-ay!*"

And if he did not care, why nobody else cared either.

But one day Tom had a new adventure. He was sitting on a water-lily leaf, he and his friend the dragon-fly, watching the gnats dance. The dragon-fly had eaten as many as he wanted, and was sitting quite still and sleepy, for it was very hot and bright. The gnats (who did not care the least for their poor brothers' death) danced a foot over his head quite happily, and a large black fly settled within an inch of his nose, and began washing his own face and combing his hair with his paws: but the dragon-fly never stirred, and kept on chatting to Tom about the times when he lived under the water.

Suddenly, Tom heard the strangest noise up the stream; cooing, and grunting, and whining, and squeaking, as if you had put into a bag two stock-doves, nine mice, three guinea-pigs, and a blind puppy, and left them there to settle themselves and make music.

He looked up the water, and there he saw a sight as strange as the noise; a great ball rolling over and over down the stream, seeming one moment of soft brown fur, and the next of shining glass: and yet it was not a ball; for sometimes it broke up and streamed away in pieces, and then it joined again; and all the while the noise came out of it louder and louder.

Tom asked the dragon-fly what it could be: but, of course, with his short sight, he could not even see it, though it was not ten yards away. So he took the neatest little header into the water, and started off to see for himself; and, when he came near, the ball turned out to be four or five beautiful creatures, many times larger than Tom, who were swimming about, and rolling, and diving, and twisting, and wrestling, and cuddling, and kissing, and biting, and scratching, in the most charming fashion that ever was seen. And if you don't believe me, you may go to the Zoological Gardens (for I am afraid that you won't see it nearer, unless, perhaps, you get up at five in the morning, and go down to Cordery's Moor, and watch by the great withy pollard which hangs over the backwater, where the otters breed sometimes), and then say, if otters at play in the water are not the merriest, lithest, gracefullest creatures you ever saw.

But, when the biggest of them saw Tom, she

darted out from the rest, and cried in the water-language sharply enough, "Quick, children, here is something to eat, indeed!" and came at poor Tom, showing such a wicked pair of eyes, and such a set of sharp teeth in a grinning mouth, that Tom, who had thought her very handsome, said to himself, *Handsome is that handsome does*, and slipped in between the water-lily roots as fast as he could, and then turned round and made faces at her.

"Come out," said the wicked old otter, "or it will be worse for you."

But Tom looked at her from between two thick roots, and shook them with all his might, making horrible faces all the while, just as he used to grin through the railings at the old women, when he lived before.   It was not quite well bred, no doubt; but you know, Tom had not finished his education yet.

"Come away, children," said the otter in disgust, "it is not worth eating, after all.   It is only a nasty eft, which nothing eats, not even those vulgar pike in the pond."

"I am not an eft!" said Tom; "efts have tails."

"You are an eft," said the otter, very positively; "I see your two hands quite plain, and I know you have a tail."

"I tell you I have not," said Tom.   "Look here!" and he turned his pretty little self quite round; and sure enough, he had no more tail than you.

The otter might have got out of it by saying that Tom was a frog : but, like a great many other people, when she had once said a thing, she stood to it, right or wrong ; so she answered :

"I say you are an eft, and therefore you are, and not fit food for gentlefolk like me and my children.  You may stay there till the salmon eat you (she knew the salmon would not, but she wanted to frighten poor Tom).  Ha ! ha ! they will eat you, and we will eat them " ; and the otter laughed such a wicked cruel laugh—as you may hear them do sometimes ; and the first time that you hear it you will probably think it is bogies.

"What are salmon ?" asked Tom.

"Fish, you eft, great fish, nice fish to eat. They are the lords of the fish, and we are lords of the salmon " ; and she laughed again. "We hunt them up and down the pools, and drive them up into a corner, the silly things ; they are so proud, and bully the little trout, and the minnows, till they see us coming, and then they are so meek all at once ; and we catch them, but we disdain to eat them all ; we just bite out their soft throats and suck their sweet juice—Oh, so good ! "—(and she licked her wicked lips)—" and then throw them away, and go and catch another. They are coming soon, children, coming soon ; I can smell the rain coming up off the sea, and then hurrah for a fresh, and salmon, and plenty of eating all day long."

And the otter grew so proud that she turned

head over heels twice, and then stood upright half out of the water, grinning like a Cheshire cat.

" And where do they come from ? " asked Tom, who kept himself very close, for he was considerably frightened.

" Out of the sea, eft, the great wide sea, where they might stay and be safe if they liked. But out of the sea the silly things come, into the great river down below, and we come up to watch for them; and when they go down again we go down and follow them. And there we fish for the bass and the pollock, and have jolly days along the shore, and toss and roll in the breakers, and sleep snug in the warm dry crags. Ah, that is a merry life too, children, if it were not for those horrid men."

" What are men ? " asked Tom; but somehow he seemed to know before he asked.

" Two-legged things, eft: and, now I come to look at you, they are actually something like you, if you had not a tail " (she was determined that Tom should have a tail), " only a great deal bigger, worse luck for us; and they catch the fish with hooks and lines, which get into our feet sometimes, and set pots along the rocks to catch lobsters. They speared my poor dear husband as he went out to find something for me to eat. I was laid up among the crags then, and we were very low in the world, for the sea was so rough that no fish would come in shore. But they speared him, poor fellow, and I saw them carrying him away upon a pole. Ah, he lost his life for your sakes, my

children, poor dear obedient creature that he
was."

And the otter grew so sentimental (for otters
can be very sentimental when they choose, like a
good many people who are both cruel and greedy,
and no good to anybody at all) that she sailed
solemnly away down the burn, and Tom saw her
no more for that time.   And lucky it was for her
that she did so; for no sooner was she gone, than
down the bank came seven little rough terrier dogs,
snuffing and yapping, and grubbing and splashing,
in full cry after the otter.   Tom hid among the water-
lilies till they were gone; for he could not guess
that they were the water-fairies come to help him.

But he could not help thinking of what the
otter had said about the great river and the broad
sea.   And, as he thought, he longed to go and see
them.   He could not tell why; but the more he
thought, the more he grew discontented with the
narrow little stream in which he lived, and all his
companions there; and wanted to get out into the
wide wide world, and enjoy all the wonderful
sights of which he was sure it was full.

And once he set off to go down the stream.
But the stream was very low; and when he came
to the shallows he could not keep under water, for
there was no water left to keep under.   So the sun
burned his back and made him sick; and he went
back again and lay quiet in the pool for a whole
week more.

And then, on the evening of a very hot day, he
saw a sight.

He had been very stupid all day, and so had the trout; for they would not move an inch to take a fly, though there were thousands on the water, but lay dozing at the bottom under the shade of the stones ; and Tom lay dozing too, and was glad to cuddle their smooth cool sides, for the water was quite warm and unpleasant.

But toward evening it grew suddenly dark, and Tom looked up and saw a blanket of black clouds lying right across the valley above his head, resting on the crags right and left.  He felt not quite frightened, but very still ; for everything was still.  There was not a whisper of wind, nor a chirp of a bird to be heard ; and next a few great drops of rain fell plop into the water, and one hit Tom on the nose, and made him pop his head down quickly enough.

And then the thunder roared, and the lightning flashed, and leapt across Vendale and back again, from cloud to cloud, and cliff to cliff, till the very rocks in the stream seemed to shake : and Tom looked up at it through the water, and thought it the finest thing he ever saw in his life.

But out of the water he dared not put his head ; for the rain came down by bucketsful, and the hail hammered like shot on the stream, and churned it into foam ; and soon the stream rose, and rushed down, higher and higher, and fouler and fouler, full of beetles, and sticks ; and straws, and worms, and addle-eggs, and wood-lice, and leeches, and odds and ends, and omnium-gatherums, and this, that, and the other, enough to fill nine museums.

Tom could hardly stand against the stream, and hid behind a rock. But the trout did not; for out they rushed from among the stones, and began gobbling the beetles and leeches in the most greedy and quarrelsome way, and swimming about with great worms hanging out of their mouths, tugging and kicking to get them away from each other.

And now, by the flashes of the lightning, Tom saw a new sight—all the bottom of the stream alive with great eels, turning and twisting along, all down stream and away. They had been hiding for weeks past in the cracks of the rocks, and in burrows in the mud; and Tom had hardly ever seen them, except now and then at night: but now they were all out, and went hurrying past him so fiercely and wildly that he was quite frightened. And as they hurried past he could hear them say to each other, "We must run, we must run. What a jolly thunderstorm! Down to the sea, down to the sea!"

And then the otter came by with all her brood, twining and sweeping along as fast as the eels themselves; and she spied Tom as she came by, and said:

"Now is your time, eft, if you want to see the world. Come along, children, never mind those nasty eels: we shall breakfast on salmon to-morrow. Down to the sea, down to the sea!"

Then came a flash brighter than all the rest, and by the light of it—in the thousandth part of a second they were gone again—but he had seen them, he was certain of it—Three beautiful little

87

white girls, with their arms twined round each other's necks, floating down the torrent, as they sang, "Down to the sea, down to the sea!"

"Oh stay! Wait for me!" cried Tom; but they were gone: yet he could hear their voices clear and sweet through the roar of thunder and water and wind, singing as they died away, "Down to the sea!"

"Down to the sea?" said Tom; "everything is going to the sea, and I will go too. Good-bye, trout." But the trout were so busy gobbling worms that they never turned to answer him; so that Tom was spared the pain of bidding them farewell.

And now, down the rushing stream, guided by the bright flashes of the storm; past tall birch-fringed rocks, which shone out one moment as clear as day, and the next were dark as night; past dark hovers under swirling banks, from which great trout rushed out on Tom, thinking him to be good to eat, and turned back sulkily, for the fairies sent them home again with a tremendous scolding, for daring to meddle with a water-baby; on through narrow strids and roaring cataracts, where Tom was deafened and blinded for a moment by the rushing waters; along deep reaches, where the white water-lilies tossed and flapped beneath the wind and hail; past sleeping villages; under dark bridge-arches, and away and away to the sea. And Tom could not stop, and did not care to stop; he would see the great world below, and the salmon, and the breakers, and the wide wide sea.

And when the daylight came, Tom found himself out in the salmon river.

And what sort of a river was it?  Was it like an Irish stream, winding through the brown bogs, where the wild ducks squatter up from among the white water-lilies, and the curlews flit to and fro, crying "Tullie-wheep, mind your sheep"; and Dennis tells you strange stories of the Peishtamore, the great bogy-snake which lies in the black peat pools, among the old pine-stems, and puts his head out at night to snap at the cattle as they come down to drink?—But you must not believe all that Dennis tells you, mind; for if you ask him:

"Is there a salmon here, do you think, Dennis?"

"Is it salmon, thin, your honour manes? Salmon?  Cartloads it is of thim, thin, an' ridgmens, shouldthering ache out of water, av' ye'd but the luck to see thim."

Then you fish the pool all over, and never get a rise.

"But there can't be a salmon here, Dennis! and, if you'll but think, if one had come up last tide, he'd be gone to the higher pools by now."

"Shure thin, and your honour's the thrue fisherman, and understands it all like a book. Why, ye spake as if ye'd known the wather a thousand years!  As I said, how could there be a fish here at all, just now?"

"But you said just now they were shouldering each other out of water?"

And then Dennis will look up at you with his

handsome, sly, soft, sleepy, good-natured, untrustable, Irish grey eye, and answer with the prettiest smile :

"Shure, and didn't I think your honour would like a pleasant answer?"

So you must not trust Dennis, because he is in the habit of giving pleasant answers : but, instead of being angry with him, you must remember that he is a poor Paddy, and knows no better; so you must just burst out laughing ; and then he will burst out laughing too, and slave for you, and trot about after you, and show you good sport if he can—for he is an affectionate fellow, and as fond of sport as you are—and if he can't, tell you fibs instead, a hundred an hour ; and wonder all the while why poor ould Ireland does not prosper like England and Scotland, and some other places, where folk have taken up a ridiculous fancy that honesty is the best policy.

Or was it like a Welsh salmon river, which is remarkable chiefly (at least, till this last year) for containing no salmon, as they have been all poached out by the enlightened peasantry, to prevent the *Cythrawl Sassenach* (which means you, my little dear, your kith and kin, and signifies much the same as the Chinese *Fan Quei*) from coming bothering into Wales, with good tackle, and ready money, and civilisation, and common honesty, and other like things of which the Cymry stand in no need whatsoever ?

Or was it such a salmon stream as I trust you will see among the Hampshire water-meadows

before your hairs are grey, under the wise new
fishing-laws ?—when Winchester apprentices shall
covenant, as they did three hundred years ago, not
to be made to eat salmon more than three days a
week; and fresh-run fish shall be as plentiful under
Salisbury spire as they are in Holly-hole at Christ-
church; in the good time coming, when folks
shall see that, of all Heaven's gifts of food, the
one to be protected most carefully is that worthy
gentleman salmon, who is generous enough to go
down to the sea weighing five ounces, and to come
back next year weighing five pounds, without
having cost the soil or the state one farthing ?

Or was it like a Scotch stream, such as Arthur
Clough drew in his " Bothie " :—

> " *Where over a ledge of granite*
> *Into a granite bason the amber torrent descended. . . .*
> *Beautiful there for the colour derived from green rocks*
>     *under;*
> *Beautiful most of all, where beads of foam uprising*
> *Mingle their clouds of white with the delicate hue of*
>     *the stillness. . . .*
> *Cliff over cliff for its sides, with rowan and pendant*
>     *birch boughs.*" . . .

Ah, my little man, when you are a big man,
and fish such a stream as that, you will hardly care,
I think, whether she be roaring down in full spate,
like coffee covered with scald cream, while the fish
are swirling at your fly as an oar-blade swirls in a
boat-race, or flashing up the cataract like silver

arrows, out of the fiercest of the foam; or whether
the fall be dwindled to a single thread, and the
shingle below be as white and dusty as a turnpike
road, while the salmon huddle together in one
dark cloud in the clear amber pool, sleeping away
their time till the rain creeps back again off the
sea.  You will not care much, if you have eyes
and brains; for you will lay down your rod con-
tentedly, and drink in at your eyes the beauty of
that glorious place; and listen to the water-ouzel
piping on the stones, and watch the yellow roes
come down to drink and look up at you with their
great soft trustful eyes, as much as to say, "You
could not have the heart to shoot at us?"  And
then, if you have sense, you will turn and talk to
the great giant of a gilly who lies basking on the
stone beside you.  He will tell you no fibs, my
little man ; for he is a Scotchman, and fears God,
and not the priest; and, as you talk with him, you
will be surprised more and more at his knowledge,
his sense, his humour, his courtesy; and you will
find out—unless you have found it out before—
that a man may learn from his Bible to be a more
thorough gentleman than if he had been brought
up in all the drawing-rooms in London.

No.  It was none of these, the salmon stream
at Harthover.  It was such a stream as you see in
dear old Bewick; Bewick, who was born and bred
upon them.  A full hundred yards broad it was,
sliding on from broad pool to broad shallow, and
broad shallow to broad pool, over great fields of
shingle, under oak and ash coverts, past low cliffs

of sandstone, past green meadows, and fair parks, and a great house of grey stone, and brown moors above, and here and there against the sky the smoking chimney of a colliery.  You must look at Bewick to see just what it was like, for he has drawn it a hundred times with the care and the love of a true north countryman; and, even if you do not care about the salmon river, you ought, like all good boys, to know your Bewick.

At least, so old Sir John used to say, and very sensibly he put it too, as he was wont to do:

"If they want to describe a finished young gentleman in France, I hear, they say of him, '*Il sait son Rabelais.*'  But if I want to describe one in England, I say, '*He knows his Bewick.*'  And I think that is the higher compliment."

But Tom thought nothing about what the river was like.  All his fancy was, to get down to the wide wide sea.

And after a while he came to a place where the river spread out into broad still shallow reaches, so wide that little Tom, as he put his head out of the water, could hardly see across.

And there he stopped.  He got a little frightened.  "This must be the sea," he thought.  "What a wide place it is !  If I go on into it I shall surely lose my way, or some strange thing will bite me.  I will stop here and look out for the otter, or the eels, or some one to tell me where I shall go."

So he went back a little way, and crept into a crack of the rock, just where the river opened out into the wide shallows, and watched for some one to tell him his way: but the otter and the eels were gone on miles and miles down the stream.

There he waited, and slept too, for he was quite tired with his night's journey; and, when he woke, the stream was clearing to a beautiful amber hue, though it was still very high. And after a while he saw a sight which made him jump up; for he knew in a moment it was one of the things which he had come to look for.

Such a fish! ten times as big as the biggest trout, and a hundred times as big as Tom, sculling up the stream past him, as easily as Tom had sculled down.

Such a fish! shining silver from head to tail, and here and there a crimson dot; with a grand hooked nose and grand curling lip, and a grand bright eye, looking round him as proudly as a king, and surveying the water right and left as if all belonged to him. Surely he must be the salmon, the king of all the fish.

Tom was so frightened that he longed to creep into a hole; but he need not have been; for salmon are all true gentlemen, and, like true gentlemen, they look noble and proud enough, and yet, like true gentlemen, they never harm or quarrel with any one, but go about their own business, and leave rude fellows to themselves.

The salmon looked at him full in the face, and then went on without minding him, with a swish or two of his tail which made the stream boil again. And in a few minutes came another, and

then four or five, and so on; and all passed Tom,
rushing and plunging up the cataract with strong
strokes of their silver tails, now and then leaping
clean out of water and up over a rock, shining
gloriously for a moment in the bright sun ; while
Tom was so delighted that he could have watched
them all day long.

And at last one came up bigger than all the
rest ; but he came slowly, and stopped, and looked
back, and seemed very anxious and busy.   And
Tom saw that he was helping another salmon, an
especially handsome one, who had not a single spot
upon it, but was clothed in pure silver from nose
to tail.

"My dear," said the great fish to his com-
panion, "you really look dreadfully tired, and you
must not over-exert yourself at first.   Do rest yourself behind this rock"; and he shoved her gently
with his nose, to the rock where Tom sat.

You must know that this was the salmon's
wife.   For salmon, like other true gentlemen,
always choose their lady, and love her, and are
true to her, and take care of her and work for her,
and fight for her, as every true gentleman ought ;
and are not like vulgar chub and roach and pike,
who have no high feelings, and take no care of
their wives.

Then he saw Tom, and looked at him very
fiercely one moment, as if he was going to bite
him.

"What do you want here?" he said, very
fiercely.

"Oh, don't hurt me!" cried Tom. "I only want to look at you; you are so handsome."

"Ah?" said the salmon, very stately but very civilly. "I really beg your pardon; I see what you are, my little dear. I have met one or two creatures like you before, and found them very agreeable and well-behaved. Indeed, one of them showed me a great kindness lately, which I hope to be able to repay. I hope we shall not be in your way here. As soon as this lady is rested, we shall proceed on our journey."

What a well-bred old salmon he was!

"So you have seen things like me before?" asked Tom.

"Several times, my dear. Indeed, it was only last night that one at the river's mouth came and warned me and my wife of some new stake-nets which had got into the stream, I cannot tell how, since last winter, and showed us the way round them, in the most charmingly obliging way."

"So there are babies in the sea?" cried Tom, and clapped his little hands. "Then I shall have some one to play with there? How delightful!"

"Were there no babies up this stream?" asked the lady salmon.

"No! and I grew so lonely. I thought I saw three last night; but they were gone in an instant, down to the sea. So I went too; for I had nothing to play with but caddises and dragon-flies and trout."

"Ugh!" cried the lady, "what low company!"

" My dear, if he has been in low company, he has certainly not learnt their low manners," said the salmon.

" No, indeed, poor little dear: but how sad for him to live among such people as caddises, who have actually six legs, the nasty things; and dragon-flies, too ! why they are not even good to eat; for I tried them once, and they are all hard and empty; and, as for trout, every one knows what they are." Whereon she curled up her lip, and looked dreadfully scornful, while her husband curled up his too, till he looked as proud as Alcibiades.

"Why do you dislike the trout so ?" asked Tom.

" My dear, we do not even mention them, if we can help it; for I am sorry to say they are relations of ours who do us no credit.  A great many years ago they were just like us : but they were so lazy, and cowardly, and greedy, that instead of going down to the sea every year to see the world and grow strong and fat, they chose to stay and poke about in the little streams and eat worms and grubs; and they are very properly punished for it; for they have grown ugly and brown and spotted and small; and are actually so degraded in their tastes, that they will eat our children."

" And then they pretend to scrape acquaintance with us again," said the lady.  " Why, I have actually known one of them propose to a lady salmon, the little impudent little creature."

" I should hope," said the gentleman, " that there are very few ladies of our race who would degrade themselves by listening to such a creature for an instant. If I saw such a thing happen, I should consider it my duty to put them both to death upon the spot." So the old salmon said, like an old blue-blooded hidalgo of Spain ; and what is more, he would have done it too. For you must know, no enemies are so bitter against each other as those who are of the same race ; and a salmon looks on a trout, as some great folks look on some little folks, as something just too much like himself to be tolerated.

"Sweet is the lore which Nature brings;
Our meddling intellect
Mis-shapes the beauteous forms of things
We murder to dissect.

Enough of science and of art:
Close up these barren leaves;
Come forth, and bring with you a heart
That watches and receives."

WORDSWORTH.

# CHAPTER IV

So the salmon went up, after Tom had warned them of the wicked old otter; and Tom went down, but slowly and cautiously, coasting along the shore. He was many days about it, for it was many miles down to the sea; and perhaps he would never have found his way, if the fairies had not guided him, without his seeing their fair faces, or feeling their gentle hands.

And, as he went, he had a very strange adventure. It was a clear still September night, and the moon shone so brightly down through the water, that he could not sleep, though he shut his eyes as tight as possible. So at last he came up to the top, and sat upon a little point of rock, and looked up at the broad yellow moon, and wondered what she was, and thought that she looked at him. And he watched the moonlight on the rippling river, and the black heads of the firs, and the silver-frosted lawns, and listened to the owl's hoot, and the snipe's bleat, and the fox's bark, and the otter's laugh; and smelt the soft perfume of the birches, and the wafts of heather honey off the grouse moor far above; and felt very happy, though he could not well tell why. You, of course, would have been very cold sitting there on a September night, without the least bit of clothes on your wet back; but Tom was a water-baby, and therefore felt cold no more than a fish.

Suddenly, he saw a beautiful sight. A bright red light moved along the river-side, and threw down into the water a long tap-root of flame. Tom, curious little rogue that he was, must needs go and see what it was; so he swam to the shore, and met the light as it stopped over a shallow run at the edge of a low rock.

And there, underneath the light, lay five or six great salmon, looking up at the flame with their great goggle eyes, and wagging their tails, as if they were very much pleased at it.

Tom came to the top, to look at this wonderful light nearer, and made a splash.

And he heard a voice say:

"There was a fish rose."

He did not know what the words meant: but he seemed to know the sound of them, and to know the voice which spoke them; and he saw on the bank three great two-legged creatures, one of whom held the light, flaring and sputtering, and another a long pole. And he knew that they were men, and was frightened, and crept into a hole in the rock, from which he could see what went on.

The man with the torch bent down over the water, and looked earnestly in; and then he said:

"Tak' that muckle fellow, lad; he's ower fifteen punds; and haud your hand steady."

Tom felt that there was some danger coming,

and longed to warn the foolish salmon, who kept staring up at the light as if he was bewitched. But before he could make up his mind, down came the pole through the water; there was a fearful splash and struggle, and Tom saw that the poor salmon was speared right through, and was lifted out of the water.

And then, from behind, there sprang on these three men three other men; and there were shouts, and blows, and words which Tom recollected to have heard before; and he shuddered and turned sick at them now, for he felt somehow that they were strange, and ugly, and wrong, and horrible. And it all began to come back to him. They were men; and they were fighting; savage, desperate, up-and-down fighting, such as Tom had seen too many times before.

And he stopped his little ears, and longed to swim away; and was very glad that he was a water-baby, and had nothing to do any more with horrid dirty men, with foul clothes on their backs, and foul words on their lips; but he dared not stir out of his hole: while the rock shook over his head with the trampling and struggling of the keepers and the poachers.

All of a sudden there was a tremendous splash, and a frightful flash, and a hissing, and all was still.

For into the water, close to Tom, fell one of the men; he who held the light in his hand. Into the swift river he sank, and rolled over and over in the current. Tom heard the men above run along, seemingly looking for him ; but he drifted down into the deep hole below, and there lay quite still, and they could not find him.

Tom waited a long time, till all was quiet ; and then he peeped out, and saw the man lying. At last he screwed up his courage and swam down to him. "Perhaps," he thought, "the water has made him fall asleep, as it did me."

Then he went nearer. He grew more and more curious, he could not tell why. He must go and look at him. He would go very quietly, of course; so he swam round and round him, closer and closer; and, as he did not stir, at last he came quite close and looked him in the face.

The moon shone so bright that Tom could see every feature; and, as he saw, he recollected, bit by bit, it was his old master, Grimes.

Tom turned tail, and swam away as fast as he could.

"Oh dear me !" he thought, "now he will turn into a water-baby. What a nasty troublesome one he will be ! And perhaps he will find me out, and beat me again."

So he went up the river again a little way, and lay there the rest of the night under an alder root; but, when morning came, he longed to go down again to the big pool, and see whether Mr. Grimes had turned into a water-baby yet.

So he went very carefully, peeping round all the rocks, and hiding under all the roots. Mr. Grimes lay there still; he had not turned into a water-baby. In the afternoon Tom went back again. He could not rest till he had found out what had become of Mr. Grimes.   But this time Mr. Grimes was gone; and Tom made up his mind that he was turned into a water-baby.

He might have made himself easy, poor little man; Mr. Grimes did not turn into a water-baby, or anything like one at all.   But he did not make himself easy; and a long time he was fearful lest he should meet Grimes suddenly in some deep pool. He could not know that the fairies had carried him away, and put him, where they put everything which falls into the water, exactly where it ought to be. But, do you know, what had happened to Mr. Grimes had such an effect on him that he never poached salmon any more.   And it is quite certain that, when a man becomes a confirmed poacher, the only way to cure him is to put him under water for twenty-four hours, like Grimes.   So when you grow to be a big man, do you behave as all honest fellows should; and never touch a fish or a head of game which belongs to another man without his express leave; and then people will call you a gentleman, and treat you like one; and perhaps give you good sport: instead of hitting you into the river, or calling you a poaching snob.

Then Tom went on down, for he was afraid of staying near Grimes: and as he went, all the vale looked sad.   The red and yellow leaves showered down into the river; the flies and beetles were all dead and gone; the chill autumn fog lay low upon the hills, and sometimes spread itself so thickly on the river that he could not see his way.   But he

felt his way instead, following the flow of the
stream, day after day, past great bridges, past boats
and barges, past the great town, with its wharfs,
and mills, and tall smoking chimneys, and ships
which rode at anchor in the stream ; and now and
then he ran against their hawsers, and wondered
what they were, and peeped out, and saw the
sailors lounging on board smoking their pipes ;
and ducked under again, for he was terribly afraid
of being caught by man and turned into a chimney-
sweep once more. He did not know that the
fairies were close to him always, shutting the
sailors' eyes lest they should see him, and turning
him aside from millraces, and sewer-mouths, and
all foul and dangerous things. Poor little fellow,
it was a dreary journey for him ; and more than
once he longed to be back in Vendale, playing with
the trout in the bright summer sun. But it could
not be. What has been once can never come over
again. And people can be little babies, even water-
babies, only once in their lives.

Besides, people who make up their minds to go
and see the world, as Tom did, must needs find it
a weary journey. Lucky for them if they do not
lose heart and stop half-way, instead of going on
bravely to the end as Tom did. For then they will
remain neither boys nor men, neither fish, flesh, nor
good red-herring : having learnt a great deal too
much, and yet not enough ; and sown their wild
oats, without having the advantage of reaping them.

But Tom was always a brave, determined, little
English bull-dog, who never knew when he was

beaten; and on and on he held, till he saw a long way off the red buoy through the fog. And then he found to his surprise, the stream turned round, and running up inland.

It was the tide, of course: but Tom knew nothing of the tide. He only knew that in a minute more the water, which had been fresh, turned salt all round him. And then there came a change over him. He felt as strong, and light, and fresh, as if his veins had run champagne; and gave, he did not know why, three skips out of the water, a yard high, and head over heels, just as the salmon do when they first touch the noble rich salt water, which, as some wise men tell us, is the mother of all living things.

He did not care now for the tide being against him. The red buoy was in sight, dancing in the open sea; and to the buoy he would go, and to it he went. He passed great shoals of bass and mullet, leaping and rushing in after the shrimps, but he never heeded them, or they him; and once he passed a great black shining seal, who was coming in after the mullet. The seal put his head and shoulders out of water, and stared at him, looking exactly like a fat old greasy negro with a grey pate. And Tom, instead of being frightened, said, " How d'ye do, sir; what a beautiful place the sea is ! " And the old seal, instead of trying to bite him, looked at him with his soft sleepy winking eyes, and said, " Good tide to you, my little man ; are you looking for your brothers and sisters ? I passed them all at play outside."

"Oh, then," said Tom, "I shall have play-fellows at last," and he swam on to the buoy, and got upon it (for he was quite out of breath) and sat there, and looked round for water-babies : but there were none to be seen.

The sea-breeze came in freshly with the tide and blew the fog away ; and the little waves danced for joy around the buoy, and the old buoy danced with them. The shadows of the clouds ran races over the bright blue bay, and yet never caught each other up ; and the breakers plunged merrily upon the wide white sands, and jumped up over the rocks, to see what the green fields inside were like, and tumbled down and broke themselves all to pieces, and never minded it a bit, but mended themselves and jumped up again. And the terns hovered over Tom like huge white dragon-flies with black heads, and the gulls laughed like girls at play, and the sea-pies, with their red bills and legs, flew to and fro from shore to shore, and whistled sweet and wild. And Tom looked and looked, and listened ; and he would have been very happy, if he could only have seen the water-babies. Then when the tide turned, he left the buoy, and swam round and round in search of them : but in vain. Sometimes he thought he heard them laughing : but it was only the laughter of the ripples. And sometimes he thought he saw them at the bottom : but it was only white and pink shells. And once he was sure he had found one, for he saw two bright eyes peeping out of the sand. So he dived down, and began scraping the sand away, and cried, "Don't hide; I do want some one to play with so much!" And out jumped a great turbot with his ugly eyes and mouth all awry, and flopped away along the bottom, knocking poor Tom over. And he sat down at the bottom of the sea, and cried salt tears from sheer disappointment.

To have come all this way, and faced so many dangers, and yet to find no water-babies! How hard! Well, it did seem hard: but people, even little babies, cannot have all they want without waiting for it, and working for it too, my little man, as you will find out some day.

And Tom sat upon the buoy long days, long weeks, looking out to sea, and wondering when the water-babies would come back; and yet they never came.

Then he began to ask all the strange things which came in out of the sea if they had seen any; and some said "Yes," and some said nothing at all.

He asked the bass and the pollock; but they were so greedy after the shrimps that they did not care to answer him a word.

Then there came in a whole fleet of purple sea-snails, floating along, each on a sponge full of foam, and Tom said, "Where do you come from, you pretty creatures? and have you seen the water-babies?"

And the sea-snails answered, "Whence we come we know not; and whither we are going, who can tell? We float out our life in the mid-ocean, with the warm sunshine above our heads, and the warm gulf-stream below; and that is enough for us. Yes; perhaps we have seen the water-babies. We have seen many strange things as we sailed along." And they floated away, the happy stupid things, and all went ashore upon the sands.

Then there came in a great lazy sunfish, as big as a fat pig cut in half; and he seemed to have been cut in half too, and squeezed in a clothes-press till he was flat; but to all his big body and big fins he had only a little rabbit's mouth, no bigger than Tom's; and, when Tom questioned him, he answered in a little squeaky feeble voice:

" I'm sure I don't know; I've lost my way. I meant to go to the Chesapeake, and I'm afraid I've got wrong somehow. Dear me! it was all by following that pleasant warm water. I'm sure I've lost my way."

And, when Tom asked him again, he could only answer, "I've lost my way. Don't talk to me; I want to think."

But, like a good many other people, the more he tried to think the less he could think; and Tom saw him blundering about all day, till the coast-guardsmen saw his big fin above the water, and rowed out, and struck a boat-hook into him, and took him away. They took him up to the town and showed him for a penny a head, and made a good day's work of it. But of course Tom did not know that.

Then there came by a shoal of porpoises, rolling as they went — papas, and mammas, and little children—and all quite smooth and shiny, because

the fairies French-polish them every morning ;
and they sighed so softly as they came by, that
Tom took courage to speak to them : but all they
answered was, " Hush, hush, hush"; for that was
all they had learnt to say.

And then there came a shoal of basking sharks,
some of them as long as a boat, and Tom was
frightened at them. But they were very lazy good-
natured fellows, not greedy tyrants, like white
sharks and blue sharks and ground sharks and
hammer-heads, who eat men, or saw-fish and
threshers and ice-sharks, who hunt the poor old
whales. They came and rubbed their great sides
against the buoy, and lay basking in the sun with
their back-fins out of water; and winked at Tom :
but he never could get them to speak. They had
eaten so many herrings that they were quite stupid ;
and Tom was glad when a collier brig came by
and frightened them all away; for they did smell
most horribly, certainly, and he had to hold his
nose tight as long as they were there.

And then there came by a beautiful creature,
like a ribbon of pure silver with a sharp head and
very long teeth; but it seemed very sick and sad.
Sometimes it rolled helpless on its side; and then
it dashed away glittering like white fire ; and then
it lay sick again and motionless.

" Where do you come from ? " asked Tom.
" And why are *you* so sick and sad ? "

" I come from the warm Carolinas, and the
sandbanks fringed with pines ; where the great
owl-rays leap and flap, like giant bats, upon the

tide. But I wandered north and north, upon the treacherous warm gulf-stream, till I met with the cold icebergs, afloat in the mid ocean. So I got tangled among the icebergs, and chilled with their frozen breath. But the water-babies helped me from among them, and set me free again. And now I am mending every day; but I am very sick and sad ; and perhaps I shall never get home again to play with the owl-rays any more."

"Oh !" cried Tom. "And you have seen water-babies ? Have you seen any near here ? "

"Yes ; they helped me again last night, or I should have been eaten by a great black porpoise."

How vexatious ! The water-babies close to him, and yet he could not find one.

And then he left the buoy, and used to go along the sands and round the rocks, and come out in the night—like the forsaken Merman in Mr. Arnold's beautiful, beautiful poem, which you must learn by heart some day—and sit upon a point of rock, among the shining sea-weeds, in the low October tides, and cry and call for the water-babies; but he never heard a voice call in return. And at last, with his fretting and crying, he grew quite lean and thin.

But one day among the rocks he found a play-fellow. It was not a water-baby, alas ! but it was a lobster; and a very distinguished lobster he was; for he had live barnacles on his claws, which is a great mark of distinction in lobsterdom, and no more to be bought for money than a good conscience or the Victoria Cross.

Tom had never seen a lobster before; and he was mightily taken with this one; for he thought him the most curious, odd, ridiculous creature he had ever seen; and there he was not far wrong; for all the ingenious men, and all the scientific men, and all the fanciful men, in the world, with all the old German bogy-painters into the bargain, could never invent, if all their wits were boiled into one, anything so curious, and so ridiculous, as a lobster.

He had one claw knobbed and the other jagged; and Tom delighted in watching him hold on to the seaweed with his knobbed claw, while he cut up salads with his jagged one, and then put them into his mouth, after smelling at them, like a monkey. And always the little barnacles threw out their casting-nets and swept the water, and came in for their share of whatever there was for dinner.

But Tom was most astonished to see how he fired himself off—snap! like the leap-frogs which you make out of a goose's breast-bone. Certainly he took the most wonderful shots, and backwards, too. For, if he wanted to go into a narrow crack ten yards off, what do you think he did? If he had gone in head foremost, of course he could not have turned round. So he used to turn his tail to it, and lay his long horns, which carry his sixth sense in their tips (and nobody knows what that sixth sense is), straight down his back to guide him, and twist his eyes back till they almost came out of their sockets, and then made ready, present, fire, snap!—and away he went, pop into the hole; and peeped out and twiddled his whiskers, as much as to say, " You couldn't do that."

Tom asked him about water-babies. " Yes," he said. He had seen them often. But he did not think much of them. They were meddlesome little creatures, that went about helping fish and shells which got into scrapes. Well, for his part, he should be ashamed to be helped by little soft creatures that had not even a shell on their backs. He had lived quite long enough in the world to take care of himself.

He was a conceited fellow, the old lobster, and not very civil to Tom; and you will hear how he had to alter his mind before he was done, as conceited people generally have. But he was so funny, and Tom so lonely, that he could not quarrel with him; and they used to sit in holes in the rocks, and chat for hours.

And about this time there happened to Tom a very strange and important adventure—so important, indeed, that he was very near never finding the water-babies at all; and I am sure you would have been sorry for that.

I hope that you have not forgotten the little white lady all this while. At least, here she comes, looking like a clean white good little darling, as she always was, and always will be. For it befell in the pleasant short December days, when the wind always blows from the south-west, till Old Father Christmas comes and spreads the great white table-cloth, ready for little boys and

girls to give the birds their Christmas dinner of
crumbs—it befell (to go on) in the pleasant
December days, that Sir John was so busy hunting
that nobody at home could get a word out of him.
Four days a week he hunted, and very good sport
he had; and the other two he went to the bench
and the board of guardians, and very good justice
he did; and, when he got home in time, he dined
at five; for he hated this absurd new fashion of
dining at eight in the hunting season, which forces
a man to make interest with the footman for cold
beef and beer as soon as he comes in, and so spoil
his appetite, and then sleep in an arm-chair in his
bedroom, all stiff and tired, for two or three hours
before he can get his dinner like a gentleman.
And do you be like Sir John, my dear little man,
when you are your own master; and, if you want
either to read hard or ride hard, stick to the good
old Cambridge hours of breakfast at eight and
dinner at five; by which you may get two days'
work out of one.  But, of course, if you find a fox
at three in the afternoon and run him till dark,
and leave off twenty miles from home, why you
must wait for your dinner till you can get it, as
better men than you have done.  Only see that, if
you go hungry, your horse does not; but give
him his warm gruel and beer, and take him gently
home, remembering that good horses don't grow
on the hedge like blackberries.

It befell (to go on a second time) that Sir John,
hunting all day, and dining at five, fell asleep every
evening, and snored so terribly that all the windows

in Harthover shook, and the soot fell down the chimneys. Whereon My Lady, being no more able to get conversation out of him than a song out of a dead nightingale, determined to go off and leave him, and the doctor, and Captain Swinger the agent, to snore in concert every evening to their hearts' content. So she started for the sea-side with all the children, in order to put herself and them into condition by mild applications of iodine. She might as well have stayed at home and used Parry's liquid horse-blister, for there was plenty of it in the stables; and then she would have saved her money, and saved the chance, also, of making all the children ill instead of well (as hundreds are made), by taking them to some nasty smelling undrained lodging, and then wondering how they caught scarlatina and diphtheria : but people won't be wise enough to understand that till they are dead of bad smells, and then it will be too late ; besides you see, Sir John did certainly snore very loud.

But where she went to nobody must know, for fear young ladies should begin to fancy that there are water-babies there ! and so hunt and howk after them (besides raising the price of lodgings), and keep them in aquariums, as the ladies at Pompeii (as you may see by the paintings) used to keep Cupids in cages. But nobody ever heard that they starved the Cupids, or let them die of dirt and neglect, as English young ladies do by the poor sea-beasts. So nobody must know where My Lady went. Letting water-babies die is as bad as

taking singing birds' eggs; for, though there are
thousands, ay, millions, of both of them in the
world, yet there is not one too many.

Now it befell that, on the very shore, and over
the very rocks, where Tom was sitting with his
friend the lobster, there walked one day the little
white lady, Ellie herself, and with her a very wise
man indeed—Professor Ptthmllnsprts.

His mother was a Dutchwoman, and therefore
he was born at Curaçao (of course you have learnt
your geography, and therefore know why); and
his father a Pole, and therefore he was brought up
at Petropaulowski (of course you have learnt your
modern politics, and therefore know why): but
for all that he was as thorough an Englishman
as ever coveted his neighbour's goods. And his
name, as I said, was Professor Ptthmllnsprts, which
is a very ancient and noble Polish name.

He was, as I said, a very great naturalist, and
chief professor of *Necrobioneopalæonthydrochthonan-
thropopithekology* in the new university which the
king of the Cannibal Islands had founded; and,
being a member of the Acclimatisation Society, he
had come here to collect all the nasty things which
he could find on the coast of England, and turn
them loose round the Cannibal Islands, because
they had not nasty things enough there to eat
what they left.

But he was a very worthy kind good-natured
little old gentleman; and very fond of children
(for he was not the least a cannibal himself); and
very good to all the world as long as it was good

to him.   Only one fault he had, which cock-
robins have likewise, as you may see if you look
out of the nursery window——that, when any one
else found a curious worm, he would hop round
them, and peck them, and set up his tail, and
bristle up his feathers, just as a cock-robin would;
and declare that he found the worm first; and that
it was his worm; and, if not, that then it was not
a worm at all.

He had met Sir John at Scarborough, or Fleet-
wood, or somewhere or other (if you don't
care where, nobody else does), and had made
acquaintance with him, and become very fond of
his children.   Now, Sir John knew nothing about
sea-cockyolybirds, and cared less, provided the
fishmonger sent him good fish for dinner; and
My Lady knew as little : but she thought it proper
that the children should know something.   For
in the stupid old times, you must understand,
children were taught to know one thing, and to
know it well; but in these enlightened new times
they are taught to know a little about everything,
and to know it all ill; which is a great deal
pleasanter and easier, and therefore quite right.

So Ellie and he were walking on the rocks,
and he was showing her about one in ten thousand
of all the beautiful and curious things which are
to be seen there.   But little Ellie was not satisfied
with them at all.   She liked much better to play
with live children, or even with dolls, which she
could pretend were alive; and at last she said
honestly, "I don't care about all these things,

because they can't play with me, or talk to me. If there were little children now in the water, as there used to be, and I could see them, I should like that."

"Children in the water, you strange little duck?" said the professor.

"Yes," said Ellie. "I know there used to be children in the water, and mermaids too, and mermen. I saw them all in a picture at home, of a beautiful lady sailing in a car drawn by dolphins, and babies flying round her, and one sitting in her lap; and the mermaids swimming and playing, and the mermen trumpeting on conch-shells; and it is called 'The Triumph of Galatea'; and there is a burning mountain in the picture behind. It hangs on the great staircase, and I have looked at it ever since I was a baby, and dreamt about it a hundred times; and it is so beautiful, that it must be true."

But the professor had not the least notion of allowing that things were true, merely because people thought them beautiful. For at that rate, he said, the Baltas would be quite right in thinking it a fine thing to eat their grandpapas, because they thought it an ugly thing to put them underground. The professor, indeed, went further, and held that no man was forced to believe anything to be true, but what he could see, hear, taste, or handle.

He held very strange theories about a good many things. He had even got up once at the British Association, and declared that apes had hippopotamus majors in their brains just as men have. Which was a shocking thing to say; for, if it were so, what would become of the faith, hope, and charity of immortal millions? You may think that there are other more important differences between you and an ape, such as being able to speak, and make machines, and know right from wrong, and say your prayers, and other little matters of that kind; but that is a child's fancy, my dear. Nothing is to be depended on but the great hippopotamus test. If you have a hippopotamus major in your brain, you are no ape, though you had four hands, no feet, and were more apish than the apes of all aperies. But if a hippopotamus major is ever discovered in one single ape's brain, nothing will save your great-great-great-great-great-great-great-great-great-great-great-greater-greatest-grandmother from having been an ape too. No, my dear little man; always remember that the one true, certain, final, and all-important difference between you and an ape is, that you have a hippopotamus major in your brain, and it has none; and that, therefore, to discover one in its brain will be a very wrong and dangerous thing, at which every one will be very much shocked, as we may suppose they were at the professor.—Though really, after all, it don't much matter; because—as Lord Dundreary and others would put it—nobody but men have hippopotamuses in their brains; so, if a hippopotamus was discovered in an ape's brain, why it would not be one, you know, but something else.

But the professor had gone, I am sorry to say,

even further than that; for he had read at the
British Association at Melbourne, Australia, in the
year 1999, a paper which assured every one who
found himself the better or wiser for the news,
that there were not, never had been, and could
not be, any rational or half-rational beings except
men, anywhere, anywhen, or anyhow; that *nymphs,
satyrs, fauns, inui, dwarfs, trolls, elves, gnomes,
fairies, brownies, nixes, wilis, kobolds, leprechaunes,
cluricaunes, banshees, will-o'-the-wisps, follets, lutins,
magots, goblins, afrits, marids, jinns, ghouls, peris,
deevs, angels, archangels, imps, bogies,* or worse, were
nothing at all, and pure bosh and wind.  And he
had to get up very early in the morning to prove
that, and to eat his breakfast overnight; but he
did it, at least to his own satisfaction.  Whereon
a certain great divine, and a very clever divine was
he, called him a regular Sadducee; and probably
he was quite right.  Whereon the professor, in
return, called him a regular Pharisee; and probably he was quite right too.  But they did not
quarrel in the least; for, when men are men of
the world, hard words run off them like water off
a duck's back.  So the professor and the divine
met at dinner that evening, and sat together on
the sofa afterwards for an hour, and talked over
the state of female labour on the antarctic con-
tinent (for nobody talks shop after his claret), and
each vowed that the other was the best company
he ever met in his life.  What an advantage it is
to be men of the world!

From all which you may guess that the

professor was not the least of little Ellie's opinion. So he gave her a succinct compendium of his famous paper at the British Association, in a form suited for the youthful mind. But, as we have gone over his arguments against water-babies once already, which is once too often, we will not repeat them here.

Now little Ellie was, I suppose, a stupid little girl; for, instead of being convinced by Professor Ptthmllnsprts' arguments, she only asked the same question over again.

" But why are there not water-babies ? "

I trust and hope that it was because the professor trod at that moment on the edge of a very sharp mussel, and hurt one of his corns sadly, that he answered quite sharply, forgetting that he was a scientific man, and therefore ought to have known that he couldn't know; and that he was a logician, and therefore ought to have known that he could not prove a universal negative—I say, I trust and hope it was because the mussel hurt his corn, that the professor answered quite sharply:

" Because there ain't."

Which was not even good English, my dear little boy ; for, as you must know from Aunt Agitate's Arguments, the professor ought to have said, if he was so angry as to say anything of the kind—Because there are not : or are none : or are none of them ; or (if he had been reading Aunt Agitate too) because they do not exist.

And he groped with his net under the weeds so violently, that, as it befell, he caught poor little Tom.

He felt the net very heavy; and lifted it out quickly, with Tom all entangled in the meshes.

"Dear me!" he cried.   "What a large pink Holothurian; with hands, too!   It must be connected with Synapta."

And he took him out.

"It has actually eyes!" he cried.   "Why, it must be a Cephalopod!   This is most extraordinary!"

"No, I ain't!" cried Tom, as loud as he could; for he did not like to be called bad names.

"It is a water-baby!" cried Ellie; and of course it was.

"Water-fiddlesticks, my dear!" said the professor; and he turned away sharply.

There was no denying it.   It was a water-baby: and he had said a moment ago that there were none.   What was he to do?

He would have liked, of course, to have taken Tom home in a bucket.   He would not have put him in spirits.   Of course not.   He would have kept him alive, and petted him (for he was a very kind old gentleman), and written a book about him, and given him two long names, of which the first would have said a little about Tom, and the second all about himself; for of course he would have called him Hydrotecnon Ptthmllnsprtsianum, or some other long name like that; for they are forced to call everything by long names now, because they have used up all the short ones, ever since they took to making nine species out of one. But—what would all the learned men say to him

after his speech at the British Association ?   And
what would Ellie say, after what he had just told
her ?

There was a wise old heathen once, who said,
" Maxima debetur pueris reverentia "—The greatest
reverence is due to children ; that is, that grown
people should never say or do anything wrong
before children, lest they should set them a bad
example.—Cousin Cramchild says it means, " The
greatest respectfulness is expected from little boys."
But he was raised in a country where little boys
are not expected to be respectful, because all of
them are as good as the President :—Well, every
one knows his own concerns best; so perhaps they
are.   But poor Cousin Cramchild, to do him
justice, not being of that opinion, and having a
moral mission, and being no scholar to speak of,
and hard up for an authority—why, it was a very
great temptation for him.   But some people, and
I am afraid the professor was one of them, interpret
that in a more strange, curious, one-sided, left-
handed, topsy-turvy, inside-out, behind-before
fashion than even Cousin Cramchild ; for they
make it mean, that you must show your respect
for children, by never confessing yourself in the
wrong to them, even if you know that you are so,
lest they should lose confidence in their elders.

Now, if the professor had said to Ellie, " Yes,
my darling, it is a water-baby, and a very wonderful thing it is; and it shows how little I know of
the wonders of nature, in spite of forty years'
honest labour.   I was just telling you that there

could be no such creatures ; and, behold ! here is one come to confound my conceit and show me that Nature can do, and has done, beyond all that man's poor fancy can imagine.  So, let us thank the Maker, and Inspirer, and Lord of Nature for all His wonderful and glorious works, and try and find out something about this one" ;—I think that, if the professor had said that, little Ellie would have believed him more firmly, and respected him more deeply, and loved him better, than ever she had done before.  But he was of a different opinion.  He hesitated a moment.  He longed to keep Tom, and yet he half wished he never had caught him ; and at last he quite longed to get rid of him.  So he turned away and poked Tom with his finger, for want of anything better to do ; and said carelessly, " My dear little maid, you must have dreamt of water-babies last night, your head is so full of them."

Now Tom had been in the most horrible and unspeakable fright all the while ; and had kept as quiet as he could, though he was called a Holothurian and a Cephalopod ; for it was fixed in his little head that if a man with clothes on caught him, he might put clothes on him too, and make a dirty black chimney-sweep of him again.  But, when the professor poked him, it was more than he could bear ; and, between fright and rage, he turned to bay as valiantly as a mouse in a corner, and bit the professor's finger till it bled.

" Oh ! ah ! yah !" cried he ; and glad of an excuse to be rid of Tom, dropped him on to the seaweed, and thence he dived into the water and was gone in a moment.

"But it was a water-baby, and I heard it speak!" cried Ellie. "Ah, it is gone!" And she jumped down off the rock to try and catch Tom before he slipped into the sea.

Too late! and what was worse, as she sprang down, she slipped, and fell some six feet, with her head on a sharp rock, and lay quite still.

The professor picked her up, and tried to waken her, and called to her, and cried over her, for he loved her very much: but she would not waken at all. So he took her up in his arms and carried her to her governess, and they all went home; and little Ellie was put to bed, and lay there quite still; only now and then she woke up and called out about the water-baby: but no one knew what she meant, and the professor did not tell, for he was ashamed to tell.

And, after a week, one moonlight night, the fairies came flying in at the window and brought her such a pretty pair of wings that she could not help putting them on; and she flew with them out of the window, and over the land, and over the sea, and up through the clouds, and nobody heard or saw anything of her for a very long while.

And this is why they say that no one has ever yet seen a water-baby. For my part, I believe that the naturalists get dozens of them when they are out dredging; but they say nothing about them, and throw them overboard again, for fear of

spoiling their theories.   But, you see the professor
was found out, as every one is in due time.   A
very terrible old fairy found the professor out ; she
felt his bumps, and cast his nativity, and took the
lunars of him carefully inside and out; and so she
knew what he would do as well as if she had seen
it in a print book, as they say in the dear old west
country; and he did it; and so he was found out
beforehand, as everybody always is ; and the old
fairy will find out the naturalists some day, and
put them in the *Times*, and then on whose side
will the laugh be ?

So the old fairy took him in hand very severely
there and then.   But she says she is always most
severe with the best people, because there is most
chance of curing them, and therefore they are the
patients who pay her best; for she has to work on
the same salary as the Emperor of China's physicians
(it is a pity that all do not), no cure, no pay.

So she took the poor professor in hand : and
because he was not content with things as they
are, she filled his head with things as they are not,
to try if he would like them better; and because
he did not choose to believe in a water-baby when
he saw it, she made him believe in worse things
than water-babies—in *unicorns, fire-drakes, manti-
coras, basilisks, amphisbænas, griffins, phœnixes, rocs,
orcs, dog-headed men, three-headed dogs, three-bodied
geryons*, and other pleasant creatures, which folks
think never existed yet, and which folks hope
never will exist, though they know nothing about
the matter, and never will ; and these creatures so

upset, terrified, flustered, aggravated, confused, astounded, horrified, and totally flabbergasted the poor professor that the doctors said that he was out of his wits for three months ; and perhaps they were right, as they are now and then.

So all the doctors in the county were called in to make a report on his case ; and of course every one of them flatly contradicted the other : else what use is there in being men of science ?   But at last the majority agreed on a report in the true medical language, one half bad Latin, the other half worse Greek, and the rest what might have been English, if they had only learnt to write it. And this is the beginning thereof—

" *The subanhypapaposupernal anastomoses of peritomic diacellurite in the encephalo digital region of the distinguished individual of whose symptomatic phænomena we had the melancholy honour (subsequently to a preliminary diagnostic inspection) of making an inspectorial diagnosis, presenting the interexclusively quadrilateral and antinomian diathesis known as Bumpsterhausen's blue follicles, we proceeded*"—

But what they proceeded to do My Lady never knew; for she was so frightened at the long words that she ran for her life, and locked herself into her bedroom, for fear of being squashed by the words and strangled by the sentence.   A boa constrictor, she said, was bad company enough : but what was a boa constrictor made of paving stones ?

" It was quite shocking !   What can they think is the matter with him ? " said she to the old nurse.

"That his wit's just addled ; may be wi' unbelief and heathenry," quoth she.

"Then why can't they say so ? "

And the heaven, and the sea, and the rocks, and the vales re-echoed—" Why indeed ? " But the doctors never heard them.

So she made Sir John write to the *Times* to command the Chancellor of the Exchequer for the time being to put a tax on long words ;—

A light tax on words over three syllables, which are necessary evils, like rats : but, like them, must be kept down judiciously.

A heavy tax on words over four syllables, as *heterodoxy, spontaneity, spiritualism, spuriosity, etc.*

And on words over five syllables (of which I hope no one will wish to see any examples), a totally prohibitory tax.

And a similar prohibitory tax on words derived from three or more languages at once ; words derived from two languages having become so common that there was no more hope of rooting out them than of rooting out peth-winds.

The Chancellor of the Exchequer, being a scholar and a man of sense, jumped at the notion ; for he saw in it the one and only plan for abolishing Schedule D : but when he brought in his bill, most of the Irish members, and (I am sorry to say) some of the Scotch likewise, opposed it most strongly, on the ground that in a free country no man was bound either to understand himself or to let others understand him. So the bill fell through on the first reading ; and the

Chancellor, being a philosopher, comforted himself with the thought that it was not the first time that a woman had hit off a grand idea and the men turned up their stupid noses thereat.

Now the doctors had it all their own way; and to work they went in earnest, and they gave the poor professor divers and sundry medicines, as prescribed by the ancients and moderns, from Hippocrates to Feuchtersleben, as below, viz.—

1. *Hellebore, to wit—*

> *Hellebore of Æta.*
> *Hellebore of Galatia.*
> *Hellebore of Sicily.*
> *And all other Hellebores, after the method of the Helleborising Helleborists of the Helleboric era. But that would not do. Bumpsterhausen's blue follicles would not stir an inch out of his encephalo digital region.*

2. *Trying to find out what was the matter with him, after the method of*

> *Hippocrates,*
> *Aretæus,*
> *Celsus,*
> *Cælius Aurelianus,*
> *And Galen.*

But they found that a great deal too much trouble, as most people have since; and so had recourse to—

    3.  *Borage.*
       *Cauteries.*

Boring a hole in his head to let out fumes, which (says Gordonius) " will, without doubt, do much good."   But it didn't.

> *Bezoar stone.*
> *Diamargaritum.*
> *A ram's brain boiled in spice.*
> *Oil of wormwood.*
> *Water of Nile.*
> *Capers.*
> *Good wine (but there was none to be got).*
> *The water of a smith's forge.*
> *Hops.*
> *Ambergris.*
> *Mandrake pillows.*
> *Dormouse fat.*
> *Hares' ears.*
> *Starvation.*
> *Camphor.*
> *Salts and senna.*
> *Musk.*
> *Opium.*
> *Strait-waistcoats.*
> *Bullyings.*
> *Bumpings.*
> *Blisterings*
> *Bleedings.*
> *Bucketings with cold water.*
> *Knockings down.*
> *Kneeling on his chest till they broke it in,*

*etc. etc.; after the mediæval or monkish
method: but that would not do. Bumpsterhausen's blue follicles stuck there still.*

Then—

4. *Coaxing.*
   *Kissing.*
   *Champagne and turtle.*
   *Red herrings and soda water.*
   *Good advice.*
   *Gardening.*
   *Croquet.*
   *Musical soirées.*
   *Aunt Sally.*
   *Mild tobacco.*
   *The Saturday Review.*
   *A carriage with outriders, etc. etc.*

After the modern method. But that would
not do.

And if he had but been a convict lunatic, and
had shot at the Queen, killed all his creditors to
avoid paying them, or indulged in any other little
amiable eccentricity of that kind, they would have
given him in addition—

The healthiest situation in England, on East-
hampstead Plain.

Free run of Windsor Forest.

The *Times* every morning.

A double-barrelled gun and pointers, and leave
to shoot three Wellington College boys a week
(not more) in case black game was scarce.

But as he was neither mad enough nor bad enough to be allowed such luxuries, they grew desperate, and fell into bad ways, viz.—

> 5. *Suffumigations of sulphur.*
>    *Herrwiggius his " Incomparable drink for madmen":*

Only they could not find out what it was.

> *Suffumigation of the liver of the fish * * ***

Only they had forgotten its name, so Dr. Gray could not well procure them a specimen.

> *Metallic tractors.*
> *Holloway's Ointment.*
> *Electro-biology.*
> *Valentine Greatrakes his Stroking Cure.*
> *Spirit-rapping.*
> *Holloway's Pills.*
> *Table-turning.*
> *Morison's Pills.*
> *Homœopathy.*
> *Parr's Life Pills.*
> *Mesmerism.*
> *Pure Bosh.*
> *Exorcisms, for which they read Maleus Maleficarum, Nideri Formicarium, Delrio, Wierus, etc.*

But could not get one that mentioned water-babies.

> *Hydropathy.*
> *Madame Rachel's Elixir of Youth.*

*The Poughkeepsie Seer his Prophecies.*
*The distilled liquor of addle eggs.*
*Pyropathy.*

As successfully employed by the old inquisitors
to cure the malady of thought, and now by the
Persian Mollahs to cure that of rheumatism.

> *Geopathy, or burying him.*
>
> *Atmopathy, or steaming him.*
>
> *Sympathy, after the method of Basil·Valen-*
> *tine his Triumph of Antimony, and Ken-*
> *elm Digby his Weapon-salve, which some*
> *call a hair of the dog that bit him.*
>
> *Hermopathy, or pouring mercury down his*
> *throat to move the animal spirits.*
>
> *Meteoropathy, or going up to the moon to*
> *look for his lost wits, as Ruggiero did*
> *for Orlando Furioso's : only, having no*
> *hippogriff, they were forced to use a*
> *balloon; and, falling into the North Sea,*
> *were picked up by a Yarmouth herring-*
> *boat, and came home much the wiser, and*
> *all over scales.*
>
> *Antipathy, or using him like " a man and a*
> *brother."*
>
> *Apathy, or doing nothing at all.*
>
> *With all other ipathies and opathies which*
> *Noodle has invented, and Foodle tried,*
> *since black-fellows chipped flints at Abbé-*
> *ville—which is a considerable time ago,*
> *to judge by the Great Exhibition.*

But nothing would do; for he screamed and cried all day for a water-baby, to come and drive away the monsters; and of course they did not try to find one, because they did not believe in them, and were thinking of nothing but Bumpsterhausen's blue follicles; having, as usual, set the cart before the horse, and taken the effect for the cause.

So they were forced at last to let the poor professor ease his mind by writing a great book, exactly contrary to all his old opinions; in which he proved that the moon was made of green cheese, and that all the mites in it (which you may see sometimes quite plain through a telescope, if you will only keep the lens dirty enough, as Mr. Weekes kept his voltaic battery) are nothing in the world but little babies, who are hatching and swarming up there in millions, ready to come down into this world whenever children want a new little brother or sister.

Which must be a mistake, for this one reason: that, there being no atmosphere round the moon (though some one or other says there is, at least on the other side, and that he has been round at the back of it to see, and found that the moon was just the shape of a Bath bun, and so wet that the man in the moon went about on Midsummer-day in Macintoshes and Cording's boots, spearing eels and sneezing); that, therefore, I say, there being no atmosphere, there can be no evaporation; and therefore, the dew-point can never fall below 71.5° below zero of Fahrenheit: and, therefore, it

cannot be cold enough there about four o'clock
in the morning to condense the babies' mesenteric
apophthegms into their left ventricles ; and, therefore, they can never catch the hooping-cough ; and
if they do not have hooping-cough, they cannot be
babies at all ; and, therefore, there are no babies
in the moon.—Q.E.D.

Which may seem a roundabout reason ; and so,
perhaps, it is : but you will have heard worse ones
in your time, and from better men than you are.

But one thing is certain ; that, when the good
old doctor got his book written, he felt considerably
relieved from Bumpsterhausen's blue follicles, and
a few things infinitely worse ; to wit, from pride
and vain-glory, and from blindness and hardness of
heart ; which are the true causes of Bumpsterhausen's blue follicles, and of a good many other
ugly things besides.   Whereon the foul flood-water
in his brains ran down, and cleared to a fine coffee
colour, such as fish like to rise in, till very fine
clean fresh-run fish did begin to rise in his brains ;
and he caught two or three of them (which is
exceedingly fine sport, for brain rivers), and
anatomised them carefully, and never mentioned
what he found out from them, except to little
children ; and became ever after a sadder and a
wiser man ; which is a very good thing to become,
my dear little boy, even though one has to pay a
heavy price for the blessing.

"Stern Lawgiver! yet thou dost wear
    The Godhead's most benignant grace;
    Nor know we anything so fair
    As is the smile upon thy face:
    Flowers laugh before thee on their beds
    And fragrance in thy footing treads;
    Thou dost preserve the stars from wrong;
And the most ancient heavens, through Thee, are fresh and strong."

WORDSWORTH, *Ode to Duty*.

# CHAPTER V

BUT what became of little Tom?

He slipped away off the rocks into the water, as I said before. But he could not help thinking of little Ellie. He did not remember who she was; but he knew that she was a little girl, though she was a hundred times as big as he. That is not surprising: size has nothing to do with kindred. A tiny weed may be first cousin to a great tree; and a little dog like Vick knows that Lioness is a dog too, though she is twenty times larger than herself. So Tom knew that Ellie was a little girl, and thought about her all that day, and longed to have had her to play with; but he had very soon to think of something else. And here is the account of what happened to him, as it was published next morning in the Waterproof Gazette, on the finest watered paper, for the use of the great fairy, Mrs. Bedonebyasyoudid, who reads the news very carefully every morning, and especially the police cases, as you will hear very soon.

He was going along the rocks in three-fathom water, watching the pollock catch prawns, and the wrasses nibble barnacles off the rocks, shells and all, when he saw a round cage of green withes; and inside it, looking very much ashamed of himself, sat his friend the lobster, twiddling his horns, instead of thumbs.

"What, have you been naughty, and have they put you in the lock-up?" asked Tom.

The lobster felt a little indignant at such a notion, but he was too much depressed in spirits to argue; so he only said, "I can't get out."

"Why did you get in?"

"After that nasty piece of dead fish."  He had thought it looked and smelt very nice when he was outside, and so it did, for a lobster: but now he turned round and abused it because he was angry with himself.

"Where did you get in?"

"Through that round hole at the top."

"Then why don't you get out through it?"

"Because I can't": and the lobster twiddled his horns more fiercely than ever, but he was forced to confess.

"I have jumped upwards, downwards, backwards, and sideways, at least four thousand times; and I can't get out: I always get up underneath there, and can't find the hole."

Tom looked at the trap, and having more wit than the lobster, he saw plainly enough what was the matter; as you may if you will look at a lobster-pot.

"Stop a bit," said Tom.  "Turn your tail up to me, and I'll pull you through hindforemost, and then you won't stick in the spikes."

But the lobster was so stupid and clumsy that

he couldn't hit the hole. Like a great many fox-hunters, he was very sharp as long as he was in his own country; but as soon as they get out of it they lose their heads; and so the lobster, so to speak, lost his tail.

Tom reached and clawed down the hole after him, till he caught hold of him; and then, as was to be expected, the clumsy lobster pulled him in head foremost.

"Hullo! here is a pretty business," said Tom. "Now take your great claws, and break the points off those spikes, and then we shall both get out easily."

"Dear me, I never thought of that," said the lobster; "and after all the experience of life that I have had!"

You see, experience is of very little good unless a man, or a lobster, has wit enough to make use of it. For a good many people, like old Polonius, have seen all the world, and yet remain little better than children after all.

But they had not got half the spikes away when they saw a great dark cloud over them: and lo, and behold, it was the otter.

How she did grin and grin when she saw Tom. "Yar!" said she, "you little meddlesome wretch, I have you now! I will serve you out for telling the salmon where I was!" And she crawled all over the pot to get in.

Tom was horribly frightened, and still more frightened when she found the hole in the top, and squeezed herself right down through it, all eyes and teeth. But no sooner was her head inside than valiant Mr. Lobster caught her by the nose and held on.

And there they were all three in the pot, rolling over and over, and very tight packing it was. And the lobster tore at the otter, and the otter tore at the lobster, and both squeezed and thumped poor Tom till he had no breath left in his body; and I don't know what would have happened to him if he had not at last got on the otter's back, and safe out of the hole.

He was right glad when he got out : but he would not desert his friend who had saved him ; and the first time he saw his tail uppermost he caught hold of it, and pulled with all his might.

But the lobster would not let go.

"Come along," said Tom ; "don't you see she is dead?" And so she was, quite drowned and dead.

And that was the end of the wicked otter.

But the lobster would not let go.

"Come along, you stupid old stick-in-the-mud," cried Tom, "or the fisherman will catch you !" And that was true, for Tom felt some one above beginning to haul up the pot.

But the lobster would not let go.

Tom saw the fisherman haul him up to the boat-side, and thought it was all up with him. But when Mr. Lobster saw the fisherman, he gave such a furious and tremendous snap, that he snapped out of his hand, and out of the pot, and safe into the sea. But he left his knobbed claw behind him ;

for it never came into his stupid head to let go
after all, so he just shook his claw off as the easier
method.  It was something of a bull, that ; but
you must know the lobster was an Irish lobster,
and was hatched off Island Magee at the mouth of
Belfast Lough.

Tom asked the lobster why he never thought
of letting go.  He said very determinedly that it
was a point of honour among lobsters.  And so
it is, as the Mayor of Plymouth found out once to
his cost—eight or nine hundred years ago, of
course ; for if it had happened lately it would be
personal to mention it.

For one day he was so tired with sitting on a
hard chair, in a grand furred gown, with a gold
chain round his neck, hearing one policeman after
another come in and sing, " What shall we do with
the drunken sailor, so early in the morning ? " and
answering them each exactly alike :

" Put him in the round house till he gets sober,
so early in the morning "—

That, when it was over, he jumped up, and
played leap-frog with the town-clerk till he burst
his buttons, and then had his luncheon, and burst
some more buttons, and then said : " It is a low
spring-tide ; I shall go out this afternoon and cut
my capers."

Now he did not mean to cut such capers as you
eat with boiled mutton.  It was the commandant
of artillery at Valetta who used to amuse himself
with cutting them, and who stuck upon one of the
bastions a notice, " No one allowed to cut capers

here but me," which greatly edified the midshipmen in port, and the Maltese on the Nix Mangiare stairs. But all that the mayor meant was that he would go and have an afternoon's fun, like any schoolboy, and catch lobsters with an iron hook.

So to the Mewstone he went, and for lobsters he looked. And when he came to a certain crack in the rocks he was so excited that, instead of putting in his hook, he put in his hand; and Mr. Lobster was at home, and caught him by the finger, and held on.

"Yah!" said the mayor, and pulled as hard as he dared: but the more he pulled, the more the lobster pinched, till he was forced to be quiet.

Then he tried to get his hook in with his other hand; but the hole was too narrow.

Then he pulled again; but he could not stand the pain.

Then he shouted and bawled for help: but there was no one nearer him than the men-of-war inside the breakwater.

Then he began to turn a little pale; for the tide flowed, and still the lobster held on.

Then he turned quite white; for the tide was up to his knees, and still the lobster held on.

Then he thought of cutting off his finger; but he wanted two things to do it with—courage and a knife; and he had got neither.

Then he turned quite yellow; for the tide was up to his waist, and still the lobster held on.

Then he thought over all the naughty things he ever had done; all the sand which he had put in the sugar, and the sloe-leaves in the tea, and the water in the treacle, and the salt in the tobacco (because his brother was a brewer, and a man must help his own kin).

Then he turned quite blue; for the tide was up to his breast, and still the lobster held on.

Then, I have no doubt, he repented fully of all the said naughty things which he had done, and promised to mend his life, as too many do when they think they have no life left to mend. Whereby, as they fancy, they make a very cheap bargain. But the old fairy with the birch rod soon undeceives them.

And then he grew all colours at once, and turned up his eyes like a duck in thunder; for the water was up to his chin, and still the lobster held on.

And then came a man-of-war's boat round the Mewstone, and saw his head sticking up out of the water. One said it was a keg of brandy, and another that it was a cocoa-nut, and another that it was a buoy loose, and another that it was a black diver, and wanted to fire at it, which would not have been pleasant for the mayor: but just then such a yell came out of a great hole in the middle of it that the midshipman in charge guessed what it was, and bade pull up to it as fast as they could. So somehow or other the Jack-tars got the lobster out, and set the mayor free, and put him ashore at the Barbican. He never went lobster-catching again; and we will hope he put no more salt in the tobacco, not even to sell his brother's beer.

And that is the story of the Mayor of Plymouth, which has two advantages—first, that of being quite true ; and second, that of having (as folks say all good stories ought to have) no moral whatsoever : no more, indeed, has any part of this book, because it is a fairy tale, you know.

And now happened to Tom a most wonderful thing ; for he had not left the lobster five minutes before he came upon a water-baby.

A real live water-baby, sitting on the white sand, very busy about a little point of rock. And when it saw Tom it looked up for a moment, and then cried, " Why, you are not one of us. You are a new baby ! Oh, how delightful!"

And it ran to Tom, and Tom ran to it, and they hugged and kissed each other for ever so long, they did not know why. But they did not want any introductions there under the water.

At last Tom said, " Oh, where have you been all this while ? I have been looking for you so long, and I have been so lonely."

" We have been here for days and days. There are hundreds of us about the rocks. How was it you did not see us, or hear us when we sing and romp every evening before we go home ? "

Tom looked at the baby again, and then he said :

" Well, this is wonderful ! I have seen things just like you again and again, but I thought you were shells, or sea-creatures. I never took you for water-babies like myself."

Now, was not that very odd ? So odd, indeed,

that you will, no doubt, want to know how it
happened, and why Tom could never find a water-
baby till after he had got the lobster out of the pot.
And, if you will read this story nine times over,
and then think for yourself, you will find out why.
It is not good for little boys to be told everything,
and never to be forced to use their own wits.
They would learn, then, no more than they do at
Dr. Dulcimer's famous suburban establishment for
the idler members of the youthful aristocracy,
where the masters learn the lessons and the boys
hear them—which saves a great deal of trouble—
for the time being.

"Now," said the baby, "come and help me, or
I shall not have finished before my brothers and
sisters come, and it is time to go home."

"What shall I help you at?"

"At this poor dear little rock; a great clumsy
boulder came rolling by in the last storm, and
knocked all its head off, and rubbed off all its
flowers. And now I must plant it again with
seaweeds, and coralline, and anemones, and I will
make it the prettiest little rock-garden on all the
shore."

So they worked away at the rock, and planted
it, and smoothed the sand down round it, and capital
fun they had till the tide began to turn. And then
Tom heard all the other babies coming, laughing
and singing and shouting and romping; and the
noise they made was just like the noise of the ripple.
So he knew that he had been hearing and seeing
the water - babies all along; only he did not

know them, because his eyes and ears were not opened.

And in they came, dozens and dozens of them, some bigger than Tom and some smaller, all in the neatest little white bathing dresses ; and when they found that he was a new baby, they hugged him and kissed him, and then put him in the middle and danced round him on the sand, and there was no one ever so happy as poor little Tom.

" Now then," they cried all at once, " we must come away home, we must come away home, or the tide will leave us dry. We have mended all the broken seaweed, and put all the rock-pools in order, and planted all the shells again in the sand, and nobody will see where the ugly storm swept in last week."

And this is the reason why the rock-pools are always so neat and clean; because the water-babies come inshore after every storm to sweep them out, and comb them down, and put them all to rights again.

Only where men are wasteful and dirty, and let sewers run into the sea instead of putting the stuff upon the fields like thrifty reasonable souls ; or throw herrings' heads and dead dog-fish, or any other refuse, into the water; or in any way make a mess upon the clean shore—there the water-babies will not come, sometimes not for hundreds of years (for they cannot abide anything smelly or foul), but leave the sea-anemones and the crabs to clear away everything, till the good tidy sea has covered up all the dirt in soft mud and clean sand, where the water-babies can plant live cockles and whelks and razor-shells and sea-cucumbers and golden-combs, and make a pretty live garden again, after man's dirt is cleared away. And that, I suppose, is the reason why there are no water-babies at any watering-place which I have ever seen.

And where is the home of the water-babies? In St. Brandan's fairy isle.

Did you never hear of the blessed St. Brandan, how he preached to the wild Irish on the wild, wild Kerry coast, he and five other hermits, till they were weary and longed to rest? For the wild Irish would not listen to them, or come to confession and to mass, but liked better to brew potheen, and dance the pater o'pee, and knock each other over the head with shillelaghs, and shoot each other from behind turf-dykes, and steal each other's cattle, and burn each other's homes; till St. Brandan and his friends were weary of them, for they would not learn to be peaceable Christians at all.

So St. Brandan went out to the point of Old Dunmore, and looked over the tide-way roaring round the Blasquets, at the end of all the world, and away into the ocean, and sighed—" Ah that I had wings as a dove!" And far away, before the setting sun, he saw a blue fairy sea, and golden fairy islands, and he said, "Those are the islands of the blest." Then he and his friends got into a hooker, and sailed away and away to the westward, and were never heard of more. But the people who would not hear him were changed into gorillas, and gorillas they are until this day.

And when St. Brandan and the hermits came to
that fairy isle they found it overgrown with cedars
and full of beautiful birds; and he sat down under
the cedars and preached to all the birds in the air.
And they liked his sermons so well that they told
the fishes in the sea; and they came, and St.
Brandan preached to them; and the fishes told the
water-babies, who live in the caves under the isle;
and they came up by hundreds every Sunday, and
St. Brandan got quite a neat little Sunday-school.
And there he taught the water-babies for a great
many hundred years, till his eyes grew too dim to
see, and his beard grew so long that he dared not
walk for fear of treading on it, and then he might
have tumbled down. And at last he and the five
hermits fell fast asleep under the cedar-shades, and
there they sleep unto this day. But the fairies took
to the water-babies, and taught them their lessons
themselves.

And some say that St. Brandan will awake and
begin to teach the babies once more: but some
think that he will sleep on, for better for worse, till
the coming of the Cocqcigrues. But, on still clear
summer evenings, when the sun sinks down into
the sea, among golden cloud-capes and cloud-
islands, and locks and friths of azure sky, the sailors
fancy that they see, away to westward, St. Brandan's
fairy isle.

But whether men can see it or not, St. Brandan's
Isle once actually stood there; a great land out in
the ocean, which has sunk and sunk beneath the
waves. Old Plato called it Atlantis, and told strange

tales of the wise men who lived therein, and of the wars they fought in the old times. And from off that island came strange flowers, which linger still about this land:—the Cornish heath, and Cornish moneywort, and the delicate Venus's hair, and the London-pride which covers the Kerry mountains, and the little pink butterwort of Devon, and the great blue butterwort of Ireland, and the Connemara heath, and the bristle-fern of the Turk waterfall, and many a strange plant more ; all fairy tokens left for wise men and good children from off St. Brandan's Isle.

Now when Tom got there, he found that the isle stood all on pillars, and that its roots were full of caves. There were pillars of black basalt, like Staffa ; and pillars of green and crimson serpentine, like Kynance ; and pillars ribboned with red and white and yellow sandstone, like Livermead; and there were blue grottoes like Capri, and white grottoes like Adelsberg; all curtained and draped with seaweeds, purple and crimson, green and brown ; and strewn with soft white sand, on which the water-babies sleep every night. But, to keep the place clean and sweet, the crabs picked up all the scraps off the floor and ate them like so many monkeys ; while the rocks were covered with ten thousand sea-anemones, and corals and madrepores, who scavenged the water all day long, and kept it nice and pure. But, to make up to them for having to do such nasty work, they were not left black and dirty, as poor chimney-sweeps and dustmen are. No ; the fairies are more considerate and just than that, and have dressed them all in the most beautiful colours and patterns, till they look like vast flower-beds of gay blossoms. If you think I am talking nonsense, I can only say that it is true; and that an old gentleman named Fourier used to say that we ought to do the same by chimney-sweeps and dust-men, and honour them instead of despising them; and he was a very clever old gentleman: but, unfortunately for him and the world, as mad as a March hare.

And, instead of watchmen and policemen to keep out nasty things at night, there were thousands and thousands of water-snakes, and most wonderful creatures they were. They were all named after the Nereids, the sea-fairies who took care of them, Eunice and Polynoe, Phyllodoce and Psamathe, and all the rest of the pretty darlings who swim round their Queen Amphitrite, and her car of cameo shell. They were dressed in green velvet, and black velvet, and purple velvet; and were all jointed in rings; and some of them had three hundred brains apiece, so that they must have been uncommonly shrewd detectives; and some had eyes in their tails; and some had eyes in every joint, so that they kept a very sharp look-out; and when they wanted a baby-snake, they just grew one at the end of their own tails, and when it was able to take care of itself it dropped off; so that they brought up their families very cheaply. But if any nasty thing came by, out they rushed upon it; and then out of each of their hundreds of feet there sprang a whole cutler's shop of

| | |
|---|---|
| *Scythes,* | *Javelins,* |
| *Billhooks,* | *Lances,* |
| *Pickaxes,* | *Halberts,* |
| *Forks,* | *Gisarines,* |
| *Penknives,* | *Poleaxes,* |
| *Rapiers,* | *Fishhooks,* |
| *Sabres,* | *Bradawls,* |
| *Yataghans,* | *Gimblets,* |
| *Creeses,* | *Corkscrews,* |
| *Ghoorka swords,* | *Pins,* |
| *Tucks,* | *Needles,* |

*And so forth,*

which stabbed, shot, poked, pricked, scratched, ripped, pinked, and crimped those naughty beasts so terribly that they had to run for their lives, or else be chopped into small pieces and be eaten afterwards. And, if that is not all, every word, true, then there is no faith in microscopes, and all is over with the Linnæan Society.

And there were the water-babies in thousands, more than Tom, or you either, could count.—All the little children whom the good fairies take to, because their cruel mothers and fathers will not; all who are untaught and brought up heathens, and all who come to grief by ill-usage or ignorance or neglect ; all the little children who are overlaid, or given gin when they are young, or are let to drink out of hot kettles, or to fall into the fire ; all the little children in alleys and courts, and tumble-down cottages, who die by fever, and cholera, and measles, and scarlatina, and nasty complaints which no one has any business to have, and which no one will have some day, when folks have common sense; and all the little children who have been killed by cruel masters and wicked soldiers; they were all there, except, of course, the babes of Bethlehem who were killed by wicked King Herod; for they were taken straight to heaven long ago, as everybody knows, and we call them the Holy Innocents.

But I wish Tom had given up all his naughty tricks, and left off tormenting dumb animals now that he had plenty of playfellows to amuse him. Instead of that, I am sorry to say, he would meddle with the creatures, all but the water-snakes, for they would stand no nonsense. So he tickled the madrepores, to make them shut up; and frightened the crabs, to make them hide in the sand and peep out at him with the tips of their eyes; and put stones into the anemones' mouths, to make them fancy that their dinner was coming.

The other children warned him, and said, "Take care what you are at. Mrs. Bedonebyas- youdid is coming." But Tom never heeded them, being quite riotous with high spirits and good luck, till, one Friday morning early, Mrs. Bedone- byasyoudid came indeed.

A very tremendous lady she was; and when the children saw her they all stood in a row, very upright indeed, and smoothed down their bathing dresses, and put their hands behind them, just as if they were going to be examined by the inspector.

And she had on a black bonnet, and a black
shawl, and no crinoline at all; and a pair of large
green spectacles, and a great hooked nose, hooked
so much that the bridge of it stood quite up above
her eyebrows; and under her arm she carried a
great birch-rod. Indeed, she was so ugly that
Tom was tempted to make faces at her: but did
not; for he did not admire the look of the birch-
rod under her arm.

And she looked at the children one by one,
and seemed very much pleased with them, though
she never asked them one question about how they
were behaving; and then began giving them all
sorts of nice sea-things—sea-cakes, sea-apples, sea-
oranges, sea-bullseyes, sea-toffee; and to the very
best of all she gave sea-ices, made out of sea-cows'
cream, which never melt under water.

And, if you don't quite believe me, then just
think—What is more cheap and plentiful than
sea-rock? Then why should there not be sea-
toffee as well? And every one can find sea-lemons
(ready quartered too) if they will look for them at
low tide; and sea-grapes too sometimes, hanging
in bunches; and, if you will go to Nice, you will
find the fish-market full of sea-fruit, which they
call " frutta di mare ": though I suppose they call
them " fruits de mer " now, out of compliment to
that most successful, and therefore most immaculate,
potentate who is seemingly desirous of inheriting
the blessing pronounced on those who remove their
neighbours' land-mark. And, perhaps, that is the
very reason why the place is called Nice, because

there are so many nice things in the sea there: at least, if it is not, it ought to be.

Now little Tom watched all these sweet things given away, till his mouth watered, and his eyes grew as round as an owl's. For he hoped that his turn would come at last ; and so it did. For the lady called him up, and held out her fingers with something in them, and popped it into his mouth; and, lo and behold, it was a nasty cold hard pebble.

"You are a very cruel woman," said he, and began to whimper.

"And you are a very cruel boy; who puts pebbles into the sea-anemones' mouths, to take them in, and make them fancy that they had caught a good dinner ! As you did to them, so I must do to you."

"Who told you that ? " said Tom.

"You did yourself, this very minute."

Tom had never opened his lips ; so he was very much taken aback indeed.

"Yes ; every one tells me exactly what they have done wrong ; and that without knowing it themselves. So there is no use trying to hide anything from me. Now go, and be a good boy, and I will put no more pebbles in your mouth, if you put none in other creatures'."

"I did not know there was any harm in it," said Tom.

"Then you know now. People continually say that to me: but I tell them, if you don't know that fire burns, that is no reason that it should not burn you ; and if you don't know that dirt breeds fever, that is no reason why the fevers should not kill you. The lobster did not know that there was any harm in getting into the lobster-pot; but it caught him all the same."

"Dear me," thought Tom, "she knows everything!" And so she did, indeed.

"And so, if you do not know that things are wrong, that is no reason why you should not be punished for them; though not as much, not as much, my little man" (and the lady looked very kindly, after all), "as if you did know."

"Well, you are a little hard on a poor lad," said Tom.

"Not at all; I am the best friend you ever had in all your life. But I will tell you; I cannot help punishing people when they do wrong. I like it no more than they do; I am often very, very sorry for them, poor things: but I cannot help it. If I tried not to do it, I should do it all the same. For I work by machinery, just like an engine; and am full of wheels and springs inside; and am wound up very carefully, so that I cannot help going."

"Was it long ago since they wound you up?" asked Tom. For he thought, the cunning little fellow, "She will run down some day: or they may forget to wind her up, as old Grimes used to forget to wind up his watch when he came in from the public-house; and then I shall be safe."

"I was wound up once and for all, so long ago, that I forget all about it."

" Dear me," said Tom, " you must have been made a long time ! "

" I never was made, my child; and I shall go for ever and ever; for I am as old as Eternity, and yet as young as Time."

And there came over the lady's face a very curious expression—very solemn, and very sad; and yet very, very sweet.  And she looked up and away, as if she were gazing through the sea, and through the sky, at something far, far off; and as she did so, there came such a quiet, tender, patient, hopeful smile over her face that Tom thought for the moment that she did not look ugly at all. And no more she did ; for she was like a great many people who have not a pretty feature in their faces, and yet are lovely to behold, and draw little children's hearts to them at once; because though the house is plain enough, yet from the windows a beautiful and good spirit is looking forth.

And Tom smiled in her face, she looked so pleasant for the moment.  And the strange fairy smiled too, and said:

" Yes.  You thought me very ugly just now, did you not ? "

Tom hung down his head, and got very red about the ears.

" And I am very ugly.  I am the ugliest fairy in the world ; and I shall be, till people behave themselves as they ought to do.  And then I shall grow as handsome as my sister, who is the loveliest fairy in the world; and her name is Mrs. Doas-youwouldbedoneby.  So she begins where I end,

and I begin where she ends; and those who will
not listen to her must listen to me, as you will see.
Now, all of you run away, except Tom; and he
may stay and see what I am going to do.  It will
be a very good warning for him to begin with,
before he goes to school.

"Now, Tom, every Friday I come down here
and call up all who have ill-used little children and
serve them as they served the children."

And at that Tom was frightened, and crept
under a stone; which made the two crabs who lived
there very angry, and frightened their friend the
butter-fish into flapping hysterics: but he would
not move for them.

And first she called up all the doctors who give
little children so much physic (they were most of
them old ones; for the young ones have learnt
better, all but a few army surgeons, who still fancy
that a baby's inside is much like a Scotch
grenadier's), and she set them all in a row; and
very rueful they looked; for they knew what was
coming.

And first she pulled all their teeth out; and
then she bled them all round : and then she dosed
them with calomel, and jalap, and salts and senna,
and brimstone and treacle ; and horrible faces they
made; and then she gave them a great emetic of
mustard and water, and no basons; and began all
over again; and that was the way she spent the
morning.

And then she called up a whole troop of foolish
ladies, who pinch up their children's waists and

toes; and she laced them all up in tight stays, so
that they were choked and sick, and their noses
grew red, and their hands and feet swelled; and
then she crammed their poor feet into the most
dreadfully tight boots, and made them all dance,
which they did most clumsily indeed; and then
she asked them how they liked it; and when they
said not at all, she let them go: because they had
only done it out of foolish fashion, fancying it was
for their children's good, as if wasps' waists and
pigs' toes could be pretty, or wholesome, or of any
use to anybody.

Then she called up all the careless nursery-
maids, and stuck pins into them all over, and
wheeled them about in perambulators with tight
straps across their stomachs and their heads and
arms hanging over the side, till they were quite
sick and stupid, and would have had sun-strokes:
but, being under the water, they could only have
water-strokes; which, I assure you, are nearly as
bad, as you will find if you try to sit under a mill-
wheel. And mind—when you hear a rumbling
at the bottom of the sea, sailors will tell you that
it is a ground-swell: but now you know better.
It is the old lady wheeling the maids about in
perambulators.

And by that time she was so tired, she had to
go to luncheon.

And after luncheon she set to work again, and
called up all the cruel schoolmasters — whole
regiments and brigades of them; and when she
saw them, she frowned most terribly, and set to

work in earnest, as if the best part of the day's
work was to come.   More than half of them were
nasty, dirty, frowzy, grubby, smelly old monks,
who, because they dare not hit a man of their own
size, amused themselves with beating little children
instead; as you may see in the picture of old Pope
Gregory (good man and true though he was, when
he meddled with things which he did understand),
teaching children to sing their fa-fa-mi-fa with a
cat-o'-nine-tails under his chair: but, because they
never had any children of their own, they took into
their heads (as some folks do still) that they were
the only people in the world who knew how to
manage children : and they first brought into
England, in the old Anglo-Saxon times, the fashion
of treating free boys, and girls too, worse than you
would treat a dog or a horse: but Mrs. Bedonebyasyoudid has caught them all long ago ; and given
them many a taste of their own rods; and much
good may it do them.

   And she boxed their ears, and thumped them
over the head with rulers, and pandied their hands
with canes, and told them that they told stories,
and were this and that bad sort of people; and the
more they were very indignant, and stood upon
their honour, and declared they told the truth, the
more she declared they were not, and that they
were only telling lies ; and at last she birched
them all round soundly with her great birch-rod
and set them each an imposition of three hundred
thousand lines of Hebrew to learn by heart before
she came back next Friday.   And at that they all

cried and howled so, that their breaths came all up through the sea like bubbles out of soda-water; and that is one reason of the bubbles in the sea. There are others: but that is the one which principally concerns little boys.   And by that time she was so tired that she was glad to stop; and, indeed, she had done a very good day's work.

Tom did not quite dislike the old lady: but he could not help thinking her a little spiteful—and no wonder if she was, poor old soul; for if she has to wait to grow handsome till people do as they would be done by, she will have to wait a very long time.

Poor old Mrs. Bedonebyasyoudid! she has a great deal of hard work before her, and had better have been born a washerwoman, and stood over a tub all day: but, you see, people cannot always choose their own profession.

But Tom longed to ask her one question; and after all, whenever she looked at him, she did not look cross at all; and now and then there was a funny smile in her face, and she chuckled to herself in a way which gave Tom courage, and at last he said:

"Pray, ma'am, may I ask you a question?"

"Certainly, my little dear."

"Why don't you bring all the bad masters here and serve them out too?   The butties that knock about the poor collier-boys; and the nailers that file off their lads' noses and hammer their fingers; and all the master sweeps, like my master Grimes?   I saw him fall into the water long ago;

so I surely expected he would have been here.
I'm sure he was bad enough to me."

Then the old lady looked so very stern that
Tom was quite frightened, and sorry that he had
been so bold. But she was not angry with him.
She only answered, " I look after them all the
week round ; and they are in a very different place
from this, because they knew that they were doing
wrong."

She spoke very quietly ; but there was something in her voice which made Tom tingle from
head to foot, as if he had got into a shoal of sea-
nettles.

"But these people," she went on, "did not know
that they were doing wrong : they were only
stupid and impatient ; and therefore I only punish
them till they become patient, and learn to use
their common sense like reasonable beings. But
as for chimney-sweeps, and collier-boys, and nailer
lads, my sister has set good people to stop all that
sort of thing ; and very much obliged to her I am ;
for if she could only stop the cruel masters from
ill-using poor children, I should grow handsome
at least a thousand years sooner. And now do you
be a good boy, and do as you would be done by,
which they did not ; and then, when my sister,
MADAME DOASYOUWOULDBEDONEBY, comes on
Sunday, perhaps she will take notice of you, and
teach you how to behave. She understands that
better than I do." And so she went.

Tom was very glad to hear that there was no
chance of meeting Grimes again, though he was a

little sorry for him, considering that he used sometimes to give him the leavings of the beer: but he
determined to be a very good boy all Saturday;
and he was; for he never frightened one crab, nor
tickled any live corals, nor put stones into the sea
anemones' mouths, to make them fancy they had
got a dinner; and when Sunday morning came,
sure enough, Mrs. Doasyouwouldbedoneby came
too.   Whereat all the little children began dancing
and clapping their hands, and Tom danced too
with all his might.

And as for the pretty lady, I cannot tell you
what the colour of her hair was, or of her eyes:
no more could Tom; for, when any one looks at
her, all they can think of is, that she has the
sweetest, kindest, tenderest, funniest, merriest face
they ever saw, or want to see.   But Tom saw that
she was a very tall woman, as tall as her sister:
but instead of being gnarly and horny, and scaly,
and prickly, like her, she was the most nice, soft,
fat, smooth, pussy, cuddly, delicious creature who
ever nursed a baby; and she understood babies
thoroughly, for she had plenty of her own, whole
rows and regiments of them, and has to this day.
And all her delight was, whenever she had a spare
moment, to play with babies, in which she showed
herself a woman of sense; for babies are the best
company, and the pleasantest playfellows, in the
world; at least, so all the wise people in the
world think.   And therefore when the children
saw her, they naturally all caught hold of her, and
pulled her till she sat down on a stone, and climbed

into her lap, and clung round her neck, and caught hold of her hands ; and then they all put their thumbs into their mouths, and began cuddling and purring like so many kittens, as they ought to have done.   While those who could get nowhere else sat down on the sand, and cuddled her feet—for no one, you know, wear shoes in the water, except horrid old bathing-women, who are afraid of the water-babies pinching their horny toes.   And Tom stood staring at them; for he could not understand what it was all about.

"And who are you, you little darling ? " she said.

"Oh, that is the new baby!" they all cried, pulling their thumbs out of their mouths; "and he never had any mother," and they all put their thumbs back again, for they did not wish to lose any time.

"Then I will be his mother, and he shall have the very best place ; so get out, all of you, this moment."

And she took up two great armfuls of babies— nine hundred under one arm, and thirteen hundred under the other—and threw them away, right and left, into the water.   But they minded it no more than the naughty boys in Struwwelpeter minded when St. Nicholas dipped them in his inkstand ; and did nor even take their thumbs out of their mouths, but came paddling and wriggling back to her like so many tadpoles, till you could see nothing of her from head to foot for the swarm of little babies.

But she took Tom in her arms, and laid him in the softest place of all, and kissed him, and patted him, and talked to him, tenderly and low, such things as he had never heard before in his life ; and Tom looked up into her eyes, and loved her, and loved, till he fell fast asleep from pure love.

And when he woke she was telling the children a story. And what story did she tell them ? One story she told them, which begins every Christmas Eve, and yet never ends at all for ever and ever ; and, as she went on, the children took their thumbs out of their mouths and listened quite seriously ; but not sadly at all ; for she never told them anything sad ; and Tom listened too, and never grew tired of listening. And he listened so long that he fell fast asleep again, and, when he woke, the lady was nursing him still.

"Don't go away," said little Tom. "This is so nice. I never had any one to cuddle me before."

"Don't go away," said all the children; "you have not sung us one song."

"Well, I have time for only one. So what shall it be ? "

"The doll you lost ! The doll you lost ! " cried all the babies at once.

So the strange fairy sang :—

*I once had a sweet little doll, dears,*
*The prettiest doll in the world ;*

166

*Her cheeks were so red and so white, dears,*
*And her hair was so charmingly curled.*
*But I lost my poor little doll, dears,*
*As I played in the heath one day ;*
*And I cried for her more than a week, dears,*
*But I never could find where she lay.*


*I found my poor little doll, dears,*
*As I played in the heath one day :*
*Folks say she is terribly changed, dears,*
*For her paint is all washed away,*
*And her arm trodden off by the cows, dears,*
*And her hair not the least bit curled :*
*Yet, for old sakes' sake she is still, dears,*
*The prettiest doll in the world.*


What a silly song for a fairy to sing !

And what silly water-babies to be quite delighted at it !

Well, but you see they have not the advantage of Aunt Agitate's Arguments in the sea-land down below.

" Now," said the fairy to Tom, " will you be a good boy for my sake, and torment no more sea-beasts till I come back ? "

"And you will cuddle me again ? " said poor little Tom.

"Of course I will, you little duck.  I should like to take you with me and cuddle you all the way, only I must not " ; and away she went.

So Tom really tried to be a good boy, and

tormented no sea-beasts after that as long as he lived; and he is quite alive, I assure you, still.

Oh, how good little boys ought to be who have kind pussy mammas to cuddle them and tell them stories; and how afraid they ought to be of growing naughty, and bringing tears into their mammas' pretty eyes!

Thou little child, yet glorious in the night
Of heaven-born freedom on thy Being's height,
Why with such earnest pains dost thou provoke
The Years to bring the inevitable yoke—
Thus blindly with thy blessedness at strife?
Full soon thy soul shall have her earthly freight,
And custom lie upon thee with a weight
Heavy as frost, and deep almost as life."

WORDSWORTH.

# CHAPTER VI

HERE I come to the very saddest part of all my story. I know some people will only laugh at it, and call it much ado about nothing. But I know one man who would not; and he was an officer with a pair of grey moustaches as long as your arm, who said once in company that two of the most heart-rending sights in the world, which moved him most to tears, which he would do anything to prevent or remedy, were a child over a broken toy and a child stealing sweets.

The company did not laugh at him; his moustaches were too long and too grey for that: but, after he was gone, they called him sentimental and so forth, all but one dear little old Quaker lady with a soul as white as her cap, who was not, of course, generally partial to soldiers; and she said very quietly, like a Quaker:

"Friends, it is borne upon my mind that that is a truly brave man."

Now you may fancy that Tom was quite good, when he had everything that he could want or wish: but you would be very much mistaken. Being quite comfortable is a very good thing; but it does not make people good. Indeed, it sometimes makes them naughty, as it has made the people in America ; and as it made the people in the Bible, who waxed fat and kicked, like horses overfed and underworked.   And I am very sorry to say that this happened to little Tom.   For he grew so fond of the sea-bullseyes and sea-lollipops that his foolish little head could think of nothing else : and he was always longing for more, and wondering when the strange lady would come again and give him some, and what she would give him, and how much, and whether she would give him more than the others.   And he thought of nothing but lollipops by day, and dreamt of nothing else by night—and what happened then ?

That he began to watch the lady to see where she kept the sweet things : and began hiding, and sneaking, and following her about, and pretending to be looking the other way, or going after something else, till he found out that she kept them in a beautiful mother-of-pearl cabinet away in a deep crack of the rocks.

And he longed to go to the cabinet, and yet he was afraid ; and then he longed again, and was less afraid ; and at last, by continual thinking about it, he longed so violently that he was not afraid at all.   And one night, when all the other children were asleep, and he could not sleep for thinking of lollipops, he crept away among the rocks, and got to the cabinet, and behold ! it was open.

But, when he saw all the nice things inside, instead of being delighted, he was quite frightened, and wished he had never come there.   And then

he would only touch them, and he did ; and then
he would only taste one, and he did ; and then he
would only eat one, and he did ; and then he
would only eat two, and then three, and so on ;
and then he was terrified lest she should come and
catch him, and began gobbling them down so fast
that he did not taste them, or have any pleasure
in them ; and then he felt sick, and would have
only one more ; and then only one more again ;
and so on till he had eaten them all up.

And all the while, close behind him, stood Mrs.
Bedonebyasyoudid.

Some people may say, But why did she not
keep her cupboard locked ?  Well, I know.—It
may seem a very strange thing, but she never does
keep her cupboard locked ; every one may go and
taste for themselves, and fare accordingly.  It is
very odd, but so it is ; and I am quite sure that
she knows best.  Perhaps she wishes people to
keep their fingers out of the fire, by having them
burned.

She took off her spectacles, because she did not
like to see too much ; and in her pity she arched
up her eyebrows into her very hair, and her eyes
grew so wide that they would have taken in all
the sorrows of the world, and filled with great big
tears, as they too often do.

But all she said was:

"Ah, you poor little dear! you are just like
all the rest."

But she said it to herself, and Tom neither
heard nor saw her.  Now, you must not fancy

that she was sentimental at all. If you do, and think that she is going to let off you, or me, or any human being when we do wrong, because she is too tender-hearted to punish us, then you will find yourself very much mistaken, as many a man does every year and every day.

But what did the strange fairy do when she saw all her lollipops eaten?

Did she fly at Tom, catch him by the scruff of the neck, hold him, howk him, hump him, hurry him, hit him, poke him, pull him, pinch him, pound him, put him in the corner, shake him, slap him, set him on a cold stone to reconsider himself, and so forth?

Not a bit. You may watch her at work if you know where to find her. But you will never see her do that. For, if she had, she knew quite well Tom would have fought, and kicked, and bit, and said bad words, and turned again that moment into a naughty little heathen chimney-sweep, with his hand, like Ishmael's of old, against every man, and every man's hand against him.

Did she question him, hurry him, frighten him, threaten him, to make him confess? Not a bit. You may see her, as I said, at her work often enough if you know where to look for her : but you will never see her do that. For, if she had, she would have tempted him to tell lies in his fright ; and that would have been worse for him, if possible, than even becoming a heathen chimney-sweep again.

No. She leaves that for anxious parents and

teachers (lazy ones, some call them), who, instead
of giving children a fair trial, such as they would
expect and demand for themselves, force them by
fright to confess their own faults—which is so
cruel and unfair that no judge on the bench dare
do it to the wickedest thief or murderer, for the
good British law forbids it—ay, and even punish
them to make them confess, which is so detestable
a crime that it is never committed now, save by
Inquisitors, and Kings of Naples, and a few other
wretched people of whom the world is weary.
And then they say, "We have trained up the child
in the way he should go, and when he grew up he
has departed from it.  Why then did Solomon
say that he would not depart from it?"  But
perhaps the way of beating, and hurrying, and
frightening, and questioning, was not the way that
the child should go ; for it is not even the way in
which a colt should go if you want to break it in
and make it a quiet serviceable horse.

Some folks may say, "Ah ! but the Fairy does
not need to do that if she knows everything
already."  True.  But, if she did not know, she
would not surely behave worse than a British
judge and jury; and no more should parents and
teachers either.

So she just said nothing at all about the matter,
not even when Tom came next day with the
rest for sweet things.  He was horribly afraid of
coming : but he was still more afraid of staying away,
lest any one should suspect him.  He was dreadfully afraid, too, lest there should be no sweets—

as was to be expected, he having eaten them all—
and lest then the fairy should inquire who had
taken them.   But, behold! she pulled out just as
many as ever, which astonished Tom, and frightened
him still more.

And, when the fairy looked him full in the
face, he shook from head to foot: however she gave
him his share like the rest, and he thought within
himself that she could not have found him out.

But, when he put the sweets into his mouth,
he hated the taste of them ; and they made him so
sick that he had to get away as fast as he could;
and terribly sick he was, and very cross and
unhappy, all the week after.

Then, when next week came, he had his share
again ; and again the fairy looked him full in the
face; but more sadly than she had ever looked.
And he could not bear the sweets : but took them
again in spite of himself.

And when Mrs. Doasyouwouldbedoneby came,
he wanted to be cuddled like the rest ; but she
said very seriously:

" I should like to cuddle you ; but I cannot,
you are so horny and prickly."

And Tom looked at himself : and he was all
over prickles, just like a sea-egg.

Which was quite natural ; for you must know
and believe that people's souls make their bodies
just as a snail makes its shell (I am not joking,
my little man ; I am in serious, solemn earnest).
And therefore, when Tom's soul grew all prickly
with naughty tempers, his body could not help

growing prickly too, so that nobody would cuddle him, or play with him, or even like to look at him.

What could Tom do now but go away and hide in a corner and cry? For nobody would play with him, and he knew full well why.

And he was so miserable all that week that when the ugly fairy came and looked at him once more full in the face, more seriously and sadly than ever, he could stand it no longer, and thrust the sweetmeats away, saying, "No, I don't want any: I can't bear them now," and then burst out crying, poor little man, and told Mrs. Bedonebyasyoudid every word as it happened.

He was horribly frightened when he had done so; for he expected her to punish him very severely. But, instead, she only took him up and kissed him, which was not quite pleasant, for her chin was very bristly indeed; but he was so lonely-hearted, he thought that rough kissing was better than none.

"I will forgive you, little man," she said. "I always forgive every one the moment they tell me the truth of their own accord."

"Then you will take away all these nasty prickles?"

"That is a very different matter. You put them there yourself, and only you can take them away."

"But how can I do that?" asked Tom, crying afresh.

"Well, I think it is time for you to go to school; so I shall fetch you a schoolmistress, who

will teach you how to get rid of your prickles."
And so she went away.

Tom was frightened at the notion of a schoolmistress ; for he thought she would certainly come
with a birch-rod or a cane ; but he comforted himself, at last, that she might be something like the
old woman in Vendale—which she was not in the
least ; for, when the fairy brought her, she was the
most beautiful little girl that ever was seen, with
long curls floating behind her like a golden cloud,
and long robes floating all round her like a silver
one.

" There he is," said the fairy ; " and you must
teach him to be good, whether you like or not."

" I know," said the little girl ; but she did not
seem quite to like, for she put her finger in her
mouth, and looked at Tom under her brows ; and
Tom put his finger in his mouth, and looked at
her under his brows, for he was horribly ashamed
of himself.

The little girl seemed hardly to know how to
begin ; and perhaps she would never have begun
at all if poor Tom had not burst out crying, and
begged her to teach him to be good and help him
to cure his prickles ; and at that she grew so
tender-hearted that she began teaching him as
prettily as ever child was taught in the world.

And what did the little girl teach Tom ?  She
taught him, first, what you have been taught ever
since you said your first prayers at your mother's
knees ; but she taught him much more simply.
For the lessons in that world, my child, have no

such hard words in them as the lessons in this, and therefore the water-babies like them better than you like your lessons, and long to learn them more and more; and grown men cannot puzzle nor quarrel over their meaning, as they do here on land; for those lessons all rise clear and pure, like the Test out of Overton Pool, out of the everlasting ground of all life and truth.

So she taught Tom every day in the week; only on Sundays she always went away home, and the kind fairy took her place. And before she had taught Tom many Sundays, his prickles had vanished quite away, and his skin was smooth and clean again.

"Dear me!" said the little girl; "why, I know you now. You are the very same little chimney-sweep who came into my bedroom."

"Dear me!" cried Tom. "And I know you, too, now. You are the very little white lady whom I saw in bed." And he jumped at her, and longed to hug and kiss her; but did not, remembering that she was a lady born; so he only jumped round and round her till he was quite tired.

And then they began telling each other all their story—how he had got into the water, and she had fallen over the rock; and how he had swum down to the sea, and how she had flown out of the window; and how this, that, and the other, till it was all talked out: and then they both began over again, and I can't say which of the two talked fastest.

And then they set to work at their lessons

again, and both liked them so well that they went on well till seven full years were past and gone.

You may fancy that Tom was quite content and happy all those seven years ; but the truth is, he was not.   He had always one thing on his mind, and that was—where little Ellie went, when she went home on Sundays.

To a very beautiful place, she said.

But what was the beautiful place like, and where was it ?

Ah ! that is just what she could not say.   And it is strange, but true, that no one can say ; and that those who have been oftenest in it, or even nearest to it, can say least about it, and make people understand least what it is like.   There are a good many folks about the Other-end-of-Nowhere (where Tom went afterwards), who pretend to know it from north to south as well as if they had been penny postmen there ; but, as they are safe at the Other-end-of-Nowhere, nine hundred and ninety-nine million miles away, what they say cannot concern us.

But the dear, sweet, loving, wise, good, self-sacrificing people, who really go there, can never tell you anything about it, save that it is the most beautiful place in all the world ; and, if you ask them more, they grow modest, and hold their peace, for fear of being laughed at ; and quite right they are.

So all that good little Ellie could say was, that it was worth all the rest of the world put together.

And of course that only made Tom the more anxious to go likewise.

"Miss Ellie," he said at last, "I will know why I cannot go with you when you go home on Sundays, or I shall have no peace, and give you none either."

"You must ask the fairies that."

So when the fairy, Mrs. Bedonebyasyoudid, came next, Tom asked her.

"Little boys who are only fit to play with sea-beasts cannot go there," she said. "Those who go there must go first where they do not like, and do what they do not like, and help somebody they do not like."

"Why, did Ellie do that?"

"Ask her."

And Ellie blushed, and said, "Yes, Tom; I did not like coming here at first; I was so much happier at home, where it is always Sunday. And I was afraid of you, Tom, at first, because— because——"

"Because I was all over prickles? But I am not prickly now, am I, Miss Ellie?"

"No," said Ellie. "I like you very much now; and I like coming here, too."

"And perhaps," said the fairy, "you will learn to like going where you don't like, and helping some one that you don't like, as Ellie has."

But Tom put his finger in his mouth, and hung his head down; for he did not see that at all.

So when Mrs. Doasyouwouldbedoneby came, Tom asked her; for he thought in his little head,

She is not so strict as her sister, and perhaps she may let me off more easily.

Ah, Tom, Tom, silly fellow! and yet I don't know why I should blame you, while so many grown people have got the very same notion in their heads.

But, when they try it, they get just the same answer as Tom did. For, when he asked the second fairy, she told him just what the first did, and in the very same words.

Tom was very unhappy at that. And, when Ellie went home on Sunday, he fretted and cried all day, and did not care to listen to the fairy's stories about good children, though they were prettier than ever. Indeed, the more he overheard of them, the less he liked to listen, because they were all about children who did what they did not like, and took trouble for other people, and worked to feed their little brothers and sisters instead of caring only for their play. And, when she began to tell a story about a holy child in old times, who was martyred by the heathen because it would not worship idols, Tom could bear no more, and ran away and hid among the rocks.

And, when Ellie came back, he was shy with her, because he fancied she looked down on him, and thought him a coward. And then he grew quite cross with her, because she was superior to him, and did what he could not do. And poor Ellie was quite surprised and sad; and at last Tom burst out crying; but he would not tell her what was really in his mind.

And all the while he was eaten up with curiosity to know where Ellie went to ; so that he began not to care for his playmates, or for the sea-palace or anything else.   But perhaps that made matters all the easier for him ; for he grew so discontented with everything round him that he did not care to stay, and did not care where he went.

" Well," he said, at last, " I am so miserable here, I'll go; if only you will go with me ? "

" Ah ! " said Ellie, " I wish I might ; but the worst of it is, that the fairy says that you must go alone if you go at all.   Now don't poke that poor crab about, Tom " (for he was feeling very naughty and mischievous), " or the fairy will have to punish you."

Tom was very nearly saying, " I don't care if she does " ; but he stopped himself in time.

" I know what she wants me to do," he said, whining most dolefully.   " She wants me to go after that horrid old Grimes.   I don't like him, that's certain.   And if I find him, he will turn me into a chimney-sweep again, I know.   That's what I have been afraid of all along."

" No, he won't—I know as much as that. Nobody can turn water-babies into sweeps, or hurt them at all, as long as they are good."

" Ah," said naughty Tom, " I see what you want ; you are persuading me all along to go, because you are tired of me, and want to get rid of me."

Little Ellie opened her eyes very wide at that, and they were all brimming over with tears.

"Oh, Tom, Tom!" she said, very mournfully —and then she cried, "Oh, Tom! where are you?"

And Tom cried, "Oh, Ellie, where are you?"

For neither of them could see each other—not the least. Little Ellie vanished quite away, and Tom heard her voice calling him, and growing smaller and smaller, and fainter and fainter, till all was silent.

Who was frightened then but Tom? He swam up and down among the rocks, into all the halls and chambers, faster than ever he swam before, but could not find her. He shouted after her, but she did not answer; he asked all the other children, but they had not seen her; and at last he went up to the top of the water and began crying and screaming for Mrs. Bedonebyasyoudid—which perhaps was the best thing to do—for she came in a moment.

"Oh!" said Tom. "Oh dear, oh dear! I have been naughty to Ellie, and I have killed her —I know I have killed her."

"Not quite that," said the fairy; "but I have sent her away home, and she will not come back again for I do not know how long."

And at that Tom cried so bitterly that the salt sea was swelled with his tears, and the tide was .3,954,620,819 of an inch higher than it had been the day before: but perhaps that was owing to the waxing of the moon. It may have been so; but it is considered right in the new philosophy, you know, to give spiritual causes for physical phenomena—especially in parlour-tables ; and, of course, physical causes for spiritual ones, like thinking, and praying, and knowing right from wrong. And so they odds it till it comes even, as folks say down in Berkshire.

"How cruel of you to send Ellie away !" sobbed Tom. "However, I will find her again, if I go to the world's end to look for her."

The fairy did not slap Tom, and tell him to hold his tongue : but she took him on her lap very kindly, just as her sister would have done ; and put him in mind how it was not her fault, because she was wound up inside, like watches, and could not help doing things whether she liked or not. And then she told him how he had been in the nursery long enough, and must go out now and see the world, if he intended ever to be a man ; and how he must go all alone by himself, as every one else that ever was born has to go, and see with his own eyes, and smell with his own nose, and make his own bed and lie on it, and burn his own fingers if he put them into the fire. And then she told him how many fine things there were to be seen in the world, and what an odd, curious, pleasant, orderly, respectable, well-managed, and, on the whole, successful (as, indeed, might have been expected) sort of a place it was, if people would only be tolerably brave and honest and good in it ; and then she told him not to be afraid of anything he met, for nothing would harm him if he remembered all his lessons, and did what he knew was right. And at last she comforted poor little Tom so much that he was quite eager to go, and wanted to set out that minute. "Only," he said, "if I might see Ellie once before I went!"

"Why do you want that?"

"Because—because I should be so much happier if I thought she had forgiven me."

And in the twinkling of an eye there stood Ellie, smiling, and looking so happy that Tom longed to kiss her; but was still afraid it would not be respectful, because she was a lady born.

"I am going, Ellie!" said Tom. "I am going, if it is to the world's end. But I don't like going at all, and that's the truth."

"Pooh! pooh! pooh!" said the fairy. "You will like it very well indeed, you little rogue, and you know that at the bottom of your heart. But if you don't, I will make you like it. Come here, and see what happens to people who do only what is pleasant."

And she took out of one of her cupboards (she had all sorts of mysterious cupboards in the cracks of the rocks) the most wonderful waterproof book, full of such photographs as never were seen. For she had found out photography (and this is a fact) more than 13,598,000 years before anybody was born; and, what is more, her photographs did not merely represent light and shade, as ours do, but colour also, and all colours, as you may see if you look at a blackcock's tail, or a butterfly's wing, or indeed most things that are or can be, so to speak. And therefore her photographs were very curious and famous, and the children looked with great delight for the opening of the book.

And on the title-page was written, "The History of the great and famous nation of the Doasyoulikes, who came away from the country of Hardwork, because they wanted to play on the Jews' harp all day long."

In the first picture they saw these Doasyoulikes living in the land of Readymade, at the foot of the Happy-go-lucky Mountains, where flapdoodle grows wild; and if you want to know what that is, you must read Peter Simple.

They lived very much such a life as those jolly old Greeks in Sicily, whom you may see painted on the ancient vases, and really there seemed to be great excuses for them, for they had no need to work.

Instead of houses they lived in the beautiful caves of tufa, and bathed in the warm springs three times a day; and, as for clothes, it was so warm there that the gentlemen walked about in little beside a cocked hat and a pair of straps, or some light summer tackle of that kind; and the ladies all gathered gossamer in autumn (when they were not too lazy) to make their winter dresses.

They were very fond of music, but it was too much trouble to learn the piano or the violin; and as for dancing, that would have been too great an exertion. So they sat on ant-hills all day long, and played on the Jews' harp; and, if the ants bit them, why they just got up and went to the next ant-hill, till they were bitten there likewise.

And they sat under the flapdoodle-trees, and let the flapdoodle drop into their mouths; and under the vines, and squeezed the grape-juice down their throats; and, if any little pigs ran about ready roasted, crying, " Come and eat me," as was their fashion in that country, they waited till the pigs ran against their mouths, and then took a bite, and were content, just as so many oysters would have been.

They needed no weapons, for no enemies ever came near their land; and no tools, for everything was readymade to their hand; and the stern old fairy Necessity never came near them to hunt them up, and make them use their wits, or die.

And so on, and so on, and so on, till there were never such comfortable, easy-going, happy-go-lucky people in the world.

" Well, that is a jolly life," said Tom.

" You think so ? " said the fairy. " Do you see that great peaked mountain there behind," said the fairy, " with smoke coming out of its top ? "

" Yes."

" And do you see all those ashes, and slag, and cinders lying about ? "

" Yes."

" Then turn over the next five hundred years, and you will see what happens next."

And behold the mountain had blown up like a barrel of gunpowder, and then boiled over like a kettle; whereby one-third of the Doasyoulikes were blown into the air, and another third were smothered in ashes ; so that there was only one-third left.

"You see," said the fairy, "what comes of living on a burning mountain."

"Oh, why did you not warn them?" said little Ellie.

"I did warn them all that I could. I let the smoke come out of the mountain ; and wherever there is smoke there is fire. And I laid the ashes and cinders all about ; and wherever there are cinders, cinders may be again. But they did not like to face facts, my dears, as very few people do ; and so they invented a cock-and-bull story, which, I am sure, I never told them, that the smoke was the breath of a giant, whom some gods or other had buried under the mountain ; and that the cinders were what the dwarfs roasted the little pigs whole with ; and other nonsense of that kind. And, when folks are in that humour, I cannot teach them, save by the good old birch-rod."

And then she turned over the next five hundred years : and there were the remnant of the Doas-youlikes, doing as they liked, as before. They were too lazy to move away from the mountain ; so they said, If it has blown up once, that is all the more reason that it should not blow up again. And they were few in number : but they only said, The more the merrier, but the fewer the better fare. However, that was not quite true ; for all the flapdoodle-trees were killed by the volcano, and they had eaten all the roast pigs, who, of course, could not be expected to have little ones.   So they had to live very hard, on nuts and roots which they scratched out of the ground with sticks.   Some of them talked of sowing corn, as their ancestors used to do, before they came into the land of Readymade ; but they had forgotten how to make ploughs (they had forgotten even how to make Jews' harps by this time), and had eaten all the seed-corn which they brought out of the land of Hardwork years since ; and of course it was too much trouble to go away and find more. So they lived miserably on roots and nuts, and all the weakly little children had great stomachs, and then died.

" Why," said Tom, " they are growing no better than savages."

" And look how ugly they are all getting," said Ellie.

" Yes ; when people live on poor vegetables instead of roast beef and plum-pudding, their jaws grow large, and their lips grow coarse, like the poor Paddies who eat potatoes."

And she turned over the next five hundred years.   And there they were all living up in trees, and making nests to keep off the rain.   And underneath the trees lions were prowling about.

" Why," said Ellie, " the lions seem to have eaten a good many of them, for there are very few left now."

" Yes," said the fairy; " you see it was only the strongest and most active ones who could climb the trees, and so escape."

" But what great, hulking, broad-shouldered

chaps they are," said Tom ; "they are a rough lot
as ever I saw."

"Yes, they are getting very strong now; for
the ladies will not marry any but the very strongest
and fiercest gentlemen, who can help them up the
trees out of the lions' way."

And she turned over the next five hundred years.
And in that they were fewer still, and stronger, and
fiercer ; but their feet had changed shape very
oddly, for they laid hold of the branches with
their great toes, as if they had been thumbs, just
as a Hindoo tailor uses his toes to thread his needle.

The children were very much surprised, and
asked the fairy whether that was her doing.

"Yes, and no," she said, smiling.  "It was only
those who could use their feet as well as their hands
who could get a good living : or, indeed, get
married; so that they got the best of everything,
and starved out all the rest ; and those who are
left keep up a regular breed of toe-thumb-men, as
a breed of short-horns, or skye-terriers, or fancy
pigeons is kept up."

"But there is a hairy one among them," said
Ellie.

"Ah !" said the fairy, "that will be a great
man in his time, and chief of all the tribe."

And, when she turned over the next five hundred
years, it was true.

For this hairy chief had had hairy children, and
they hairier children still ; and every one wished
to marry hairy husbands, and have hairy children
too ; for the climate was growing so damp that

none but the hairy ones could live : all the rest coughed and sneezed, and had sore throats, and went into consumptions, before they could grow up to be men and women.

Then the fairy turned over the next five hundred years. And they were fewer still.

"Why, there is one on the ground picking up roots," said Ellie, "and he cannot walk upright."

No more he could ; for in the same way that the shape of their feet had altered, the shape of their backs had altered also.

"Why," cried Tom, "I declare they are all apes."

"Something fearfully like it, poor foolish creatures," said the fairy. "They are grown so stupid now, that they can hardly think : for none of them have used their wits for many hundred years. They have almost forgotten, too, how to talk. For each stupid child forgot some of the words it heard from its stupid parents, and had not wits enough to make fresh words for itself. Beside, they are grown so fierce and suspicious and brutal that they keep out of each other's way, and mope and sulk in the dark forests, never hearing each other's voice, till they have forgotten almost what speech is like. I am afraid they will all be apes very soon, and all by doing only what they liked."

And in the next five hundred years they were all dead and gone, by bad food and wild beasts and hunters ; all except one tremendous old fellow with jaws like a jack, who stood full seven feet high ; and M. Du Chaillu came up to him, and shot him,

as he stood roaring and thumping his breast.  And
he remembered that his ancestors had once been
men, and tried to say, "Am I not a man and a
brother ? " but had forgotten how to use his
tongue ; and then he had tried to call for a doctor,
but he had forgotten the word for one.  So all he
said was " Ubboboo ! " and died.

And that was the end of the great and jolly
nation of the Doasyoulikes.  And, when Tom and
Ellie came to the end of the book, they looked
very sad and solemn ; and they had good reason so
to do, for they really fancied that the men were
apes, and never thought, in their simplicity, of
asking whether the creatures had hippopotamus
majors in their brains or not; in which case, as
you have been told already, they could not possibly
have been apes, though they were more apish than
the apes of all aperies.

" But could you not have saved them from
becoming apes ? " said little Ellie, at last.

" At first, my dear; if only they would have
behaved like men, and set to work to do what they
did not like.  But the longer they waited, and
behaved like the dumb beasts, who only do what
they like, the stupider and clumsier they grew;
till at last they were past all cure, for they had
thrown their own wits away.  It is such things as
this that help to make me so ugly, that I know
not when I shall grow fair."

" And where are they all now ? " asked Ellie.

" Exactly where they ought to be, my dear."

" Yes ! " said the fairy, solemnly, half to herself,

as she closed the wonderful book. "Folks say now that I can make beasts into men, by circumstance, and selection, and competition, and so forth. Well, perhaps they are right ; and perhaps, again, they are wrong. That is one of the seven things which I am forbidden to tell, till the coming of the Cocqcigrues ; and, at all events, it is no concern of theirs. Whatever their ancestors were, men they are ; and I advise them to behave as such, and act accordingly. But let them recollect this, that there are two sides to every question, and a downhill as well as an uphill road ; and, if I can turn beasts into men, I can, by the same laws of circumstance, and selection, and competition, turn men into beasts. You were very near being turned into a beast once or twice, little Tom. Indeed, if you had not made up your mind to go on this journey, and see the world, like an Englishman, I am not sure but that you would have ended as an eft in a pond."

"Oh, dear me ! " said Tom ; " sooner than that, and be all over slime, I'll go this minute, if it is to the world's end."

"And Nature, the old Nurse, took
    The child upon her knee,
Saying, 'Here is a story book
    Thy father hath written for thee.

"'Come wander with me,' she said,
    'Into regions yet untrod,
And read what is still unread
    In the Manuscripts of God.'

"And he wandered away and away
    With Nature, the dear old Nurse,
Who sang to him night and day
    The rhymes of the universe."

LONGFELLOW.

# CHAPTER VII

"Now," said Tom, "I am ready to be off, if it's to the world's end."

"Ah!" said the fairy, "that is a brave, good boy. But you must go farther than the world's end, if you want to find Mr. Grimes; for he is at the Other-end-of-Nowhere. You must go to Shiny Wall, and through the white gate that never was opened; and then you will come to Peacepool, and Mother Carey's Haven, where the good whales go when they die. And there Mother Carey will tell you the way to the Other-end-of-Nowhere, and there you will find Mr. Grimes."

"Oh, dear!" said Tom. "But I do not know my way to Shiny Wall, or where it is at all."

"Little boys must take the trouble to find out things for themselves, or they will never grow to be men; so that you must ask all the beasts in the sea and the birds in the air, and if you have been good to them, some of them will tell you the way to Shiny Wall."

"Well," said Tom, "it will be a long journey, so I had better start at once. Good-bye, Miss Ellie; you know I am getting a big boy, and I must go out and see the world."

"I know you must," said Ellie; "but you will not forget me, Tom. I shall wait here till you come."

And she shook hands with him, and bade him good-bye. Tom longed very much again to kiss her; but he thought it would not be respectful, considering she was a lady born; so he promised not to forget her: but his little whirl-about of a head was so full of the notion of going out to see the world, that it forgot her in five minutes: however, though his head forgot her, I am glad to say his heart did not.

So he asked all the beasts in the sea, and all the birds in the air, but none of them knew the way to Shiny Wall. For why? He was still too far down south.

Then he met a ship, far larger than he had ever seen—a gallant ocean-steamer, with a long cloud of smoke trailing behind; and he wondered how she went on without sails, and swam up to her to see. A school of dolphins were running races round and round her, going three feet for her one, and Tom asked them the way to Shiny Wall: but they did not know. Then he tried to find out how she moved, and at last he saw her screw, and was so delighted with it that he played under her quarter all day, till he nearly had his nose knocked off by the fans, and thought it time to move. Then he watched the sailors upon deck, and the ladies, with their bonnets and parasols: but none of them could see him, because their eyes were not opened,—as, indeed, most people's eyes are not.

At last there came out into the quarter-gallery a very pretty lady, in deep black widow's weeds, and in her arms a baby.  She leaned over the quarter-gallery, and looked back and back toward England far away; and as she looked she sang:

### I.

" *Soft soft wind, from out the sweet south sliding,*
*Waft thy silver cloud-webs athwart the summer sea;*
  *Thin thin threads of mist on dewy fingers twining*
*Weave a veil of dappled gauze to shade my babe and*
    *me.*

### II.

" *Deep deep Love, within thine own abyss abiding,*
*Pour Thyself abroad, O Lord, on earth and air and*
    *sea;*
  *Worn weary hearts within Thy holy temple hiding,*
*Shield from sorrow, sin, and shame my helpless babe*
    *and me.*"

Her voice was so soft and low, and the music of the air so sweet, that Tom could have listened to it all day.  But as she held the baby over the gallery rail, to show it the dolphins leaping and the water gurgling in the ship's wake, lo ! and behold, the baby saw Tom.

He was quite sure of that; for when their eyes met, the baby smiled and held out his hands ; and Tom smiled and held out his hands too ; and the baby kicked and leaped, as if it wanted to jump overboard to him.

"What do you see, my darling?" said the lady; and her eyes followed the baby's till she too caught sight of Tom, swimming about among the foam-beads below.

She gave a little shriek and start; and then she said, quite quietly, "Babies in the sea? Well, perhaps it is the happiest place for them"; and waved her hand to Tom, and cried, "Wait a little, darling, only a little: and perhaps we shall go with you and be at rest."

And at that an old nurse, all in black, came out and talked to her, and drew her in. And Tom turned away northward, sad and wondering; and watched the great steamer slide away into the dusk, and the lights on board peep out one by one, and die out again, and the long bar of smoke fade away into the evening mist, till all was out of sight.

And he swam northward again, day after day, till at last he met the King of the Herrings, with a curry-comb growing out of his nose, and a sprat in his mouth for a cigar, and asked him the way to Shiny Wall; so he bolted his sprat head foremost, and said:

"If I were you, young gentleman, I should go to the Allalonestone, and ask the last of the Gairfowl.  She is of a very ancient clan, very nearly as ancient as my own; and knows a good deal which these modern upstarts don't, as ladies of old houses are likely to do."

Tom asked his way to her, and the King of the Herrings told him very kindly, for he was a

courteous old gentleman of the old school, though
he was horribly ugly, and strangely bedizened too,
like the old dandies who lounge in the club-house
windows.

But just as Tom had thanked him and set off,
he called after him: "Hi! I say, can you fly?"

"I never tried," says Tom.  "Why?"

"Because, if you can, I should advise you to
say nothing to the old lady about it.  There; take
a hint.  Good-bye."

And away Tom went for seven days and seven
nights due north-west, till he came to a great codbank, the like of which he never saw before.  The
great cod lay below in tens of thousands, and
gobbled shell-fish all day long; and the blue
sharks roved about in hundreds, and gobbled them
when they came up.  So they ate, and ate, and ate
each other, as they had done since the making of
the world; for no man had come here yet to catch
them, and find out how rich old Mother Carey is.

And there he saw the last of the Gairfowl,
standing up on the Allalonestone, all alone.  And
a very grand old lady she was, full three feet high,
and bolt upright, like some old Highland chief-
tainess.  She had on a black velvet gown, and a
white pinner and apron, and a very high bridge to
her nose (which is a sure mark of high breeding),
and a large pair of white spectacles on it, which
made her look rather odd: but it was the ancient
fashion of her house.

And instead of wings, she had two little feathery
arms, with which she fanned herself, and complained

of the dreadful heat ; and she kept on crooning an old song to herself, which she learnt when she was a little baby-bird, long ago—

"*Two little birds they sat on a stone,*
*One swam away, and then there was one,*
*With a fal-lal-la-lady.*

"*The other swam after, and then there was none,*
*And so the poor stone was left all alone;*
*With a fal-lal-la-lady.*"

It was "flew" away, properly, and not "swam" away : but, as she could not fly, she had a right to alter it. However, it was a very fit song for her to sing, because she was a lady herself.

Tom came up to her very humbly, and made his bow ; and the first thing she said was—

"Have you wings ?   Can you fly ? "

"Oh dear, no, ma'am ; I should not think of such thing," said cunning little Tom.

"Then I shall have great pleasure in talking to you, my dear.   It is quite refreshing nowadays to see anything without wings.   They must all have wings, forsooth, now, every new upstart sort of bird, and fly.   What can they want with flying, and raising themselves above their proper station in life ?   In the days of my ancestors no birds ever thought of having wings, and did very well without ; and now they all laugh at me because I keep to the good old fashion.   Why, the very marrocks and dovekies have got wings, the vulgar creatures,

and poor little ones enough they are; and my own
cousins too, the razor-bills, who are gentlefolk
born, and ought to know better than to ape their
inferiors."

And so she was running on, while Tom tried
to get in a word edgeways; and at last he did,
when the old lady got out of breath, and began
fanning herself again; and then he asked if she
knew the way to Shiny Wall.

"Shiny Wall ?   Who should know better than
I ?   We all came from Shiny Wall, thousands of
years ago, when it was decently cold, and the
climate was fit for gentlefolk; but now, what with
the heat, and what with these vulgar-winged things
who fly up and down and eat everything, so that
gentlepeople's hunting is all spoilt, and one really
cannot get one's living, or hardly venture off the
rock for fear of being flown against by some creature
that would not have dared to come within a mile
of one a thousand years ago—what was I saying?
Why, we have quite gone down in the world, my
dear, and have nothing left but our honour.   And
I am the last of my family.   A friend of mine and
I came and settled on this rock when we were
young, to be out of the way of low people.   Once
we were a great nation, and spread over all the
Northern Isles.   But men shot us so, and knocked
us on the head, and took our eggs—why, if you
will believe it, they say that on the coast of
Labrador the sailors used to lay a plank from the
rock on board the thing called their ship, and drive
us along the plank by hundreds, till we tumbled

down into the ship's waist in heaps; and then, I suppose, they ate us, the nasty fellows! Well—but—what was I saying? At last, there were none of us left, except on the old Gairfowlskerry, just off the Iceland coast, up which no man could climb. Even there we had no peace; for one day, when I was quite a young girl, the land rocked, and the sea boiled, and the sky grew dark, and all the air was filled with smoke and dust, and down tumbled the old Gairfowlskerry into the sea. The dovekies and marrocks, of course, all flew away; but we were too proud to do that. Some of us were dashed to pieces, and some drowned; and those who were left got away to Eldey, and the dovekies tell me they are all dead now, and that another Gairfowlskerry has risen out of the sea close to the old one, but that it is such a poor flat place that it is not safe to live on: and so here I am left alone."

This was the Gairfowl's story, and, strange as it may seem, it is every word of it true.

"If you only had had wings!" said Tom; "then you might all have flown away too."

"Yes, young gentleman: and if people are not gentlemen and ladies, and forget that *noblesse oblige*, they will find it as easy to get on in the world as other people who don't care what they do. Why, if I had not recollected that *noblesse oblige*, I should not have been all alone now." And the poor old lady sighed.

"How was that, ma'am?"

"Why, my dear, a gentleman came hither with

me, and after we had been here some time, he
wanted to marry—in fact, he actually proposed to
me.  Well, I can't blame him; I was young, and
very handsome then, I don't deny: but you see, I
could not hear of such a thing, because he was my
deceased sister's husband, you see?"

"Of course not, ma'am," said Tom; though,
of course, he knew nothing about it.  "She was
very much diseased, I suppose?"

"You do not understand me, my dear.  I
mean, that being a lady, and with right and
honourable feelings, as our house always has had,
I felt it my duty to snub him, and howk him, and
peck him continually, to keep him at his proper
distance; and, to tell the truth, I once pecked him
a little too hard, poor fellow, and he tumbled
backwards off the rock, and—really, it was very
unfortunate, but it was not my fault—a shark
coming by saw him flapping, and snapped him up.
And since then I have lived all alone—

        '*With a fal-lal-la-lady.*'

And soon I shall be gone, my little dear, and
nobody will miss me ; and then the poor stone
will be left all alone."

"But, please, which is the way to Shiny
Wall?" said Tom.

"Oh, you must go, my little dear—you must
go.  Let me see—I am sure—that is—really, my
poor old brains are getting quite puzzled.  Do
you know, my little dear, I am afraid, if you want

to know, you must ask some of these vulgar birds about, for I have quite forgotten."

And the poor old Gairfowl began to cry tears of pure oil; and Tom was quite sorry for her; and for himself too, for he was at his wit's end whom to ask.

But by there came a flock of petrels, who are Mother Carey's own chickens; and Tom thought them much prettier than Lady Gairfowl, and so perhaps they were; for Mother Carey had had a great deal of fresh experience between the time that she invented the Gairfowl and the time that she invented them. They flitted along like a flock of black swallows, and hopped and skipped from wave to wave, lifting up their little feet behind them so daintily, and whistling to each other so tenderly, that Tom fell in love with them at once, and called them to know the way to Shiny Wall.

"Shiny Wall? Do you want Shiny Wall? Then come with us, and we will show you. We are Mother Carey's own chickens, and she sends us out over all the seas, to show the good birds the way home."

Tom was delighted, and swam off to them, after he had made his bow to the Gairfowl. But she would not return his bow : but held herself bolt upright, and wept tears of oil as she sang :

> " *And so the poor stone was left all alone;*
> *With a fal-lal-la-lady*."

But she was wrong there ; for the stone was

not left all alone : and the next time that Tom goes by it, he will see a sight worth seeing.

The old Gairfowl is gone already : but there are better things come in her place ; and when Tom comes he will see the fishing-smacks anchored there in hundreds, from Scotland, and from Ireland, and from the Orkneys, and the Shetlands, and from all the Northern ports, full of the children of the old Norse Vikings, the masters of the sea. And the men will be hauling in the great cod by thousands, till their hands are sore from the lines; and they will be making cod-liver oil and guano, and salting down the fish ; and there will be a man-of-war steamer there to protect them, and a lighthouse to show them the way ; and you and I, perhaps, shall go some day to the Allalonestone to the great summer sea-fair, and dredge strange creatures such as man never saw before ; and we shall hear the sailors boast that it is not the worst jewel in Queen Victoria's crown, for there are eighty miles of codbank, and food for all the poor folk in the land. That is what Tom will see, and perhaps you and I shall see it too. And then we shall not be sorry because we cannot get a Gairfowl to stuff, much less find gairfowl enough to drive them into stone pens and slaughter them, as the old Norsemen did, or drive them on board along a plank till the ship was victualled with them, as the old English and French rovers used to do, of whom dear old Hakluyt tells : but we shall remember what Mr. Tennyson says : how

*" The old order changeth, giving place to the new,*
   *And God fulfils himself in many ways."*

And now Tom was all agog to start for Shiny
Wall; but the petrels said no. They must go
first to Allfowlsness, and wait there for the great
gathering of all the sea-birds, before they start for
their summer breeding-places far away in the
Northern Isles; and there they would be sure to
find some birds which were going to Shiny Wall:
but where Allfowlsness was, he must promise never
to tell, lest men should go there and shoot the
birds, and stuff them, and put them into stupid
museums, instead of leaving them to play and
breed and work in Mother Carey's water-garden,
where they ought to be.

So where Allfowlsness is nobody must know;
and all that is to be said about it is, that Tom
waited there many days; and as he waited, he saw
a very curious sight. On the rabbit burrows on
the shore there gathered hundreds and hundreds
of hoodie-crows, such as you see in Cambridge-
shire. And they made such a noise, that Tom
came on shore and went up to see what was the
matter.

And there he found them holding their great
caucus, which they hold every year in the North;
and all their stump-orators were speechifying; and
for a tribune, the speaker stood on an old sheep's
skull.

And they cawed and cawed, and boasted of all
the clever things they had done; how many lambs'

eyes they had picked out, and how many dead
bullocks they had eaten, and how many young
grouse they had swallowed whole, and how many
grouse-eggs they had flown away with, stuck on
the point of their bills, which is the hoodie-crow's
particularly clever feat, of which he is as proud as
a gipsy is of doing the hokanybaro; and what that
is, I won't tell you.

And at last they brought out the prettiest,
neatest young lady-crow that ever was seen, and
set her in the middle, and all began abusing and
vilifying, and rating, and bullyragging at her,
because she had stolen no grouse-eggs, and had
actually dared to say that she would not steal any.
So she was to be tried publicly by their laws (for
the hoodies always try some offenders in their
great yearly parliament). And there she stood in
the middle, in her black gown and grey hood,
looking as meek and as neat as a Quakeress, and
they all bawled at her at once—

And it was in vain that she pleaded—

*That she did not like grouse-eggs;*
*That she could get her living very well without*
*them;*
*That she was afraid to eat them, for fear of the*
*gamekeepers;*
*That she had not the heart to eat them, because the*
*grouse were such pretty, kind, jolly birds;*
*And a dozen reasons more.*

For all the other scaul-crows set upon her, and
pecked her to death there and then, before Tom

could come to help her ; and then flew away, very proud of what they had done.

Now, was not this a scandalous transaction ?

But they are true republicans, these hoodies, who do every one just what he likes, and make other people do so too; so that, for any freedom of speech, thought, or action, which is allowed among them, they might as well be American citizens of the new school.

But the fairies took the good crow, and gave her nine new sets of feathers running, and turned her at last into the most beautiful bird of paradise with a green velvet suit and a long tail, and sent her to eat fruit in the Spice Islands, where cloves and nutmegs grow.

And Mrs. Bedonebyasyoudid settled her account with the wicked hoodies. For, as they flew away, what should they find but a nasty dead dog ?—on which they all set to work, pecking and gobbling and cawing and quarrelling to their hearts' content. But the moment afterwards, they all threw up their bills into the air, and gave one screech ; and then turned head over heels backward, and fell down dead, one hundred and twenty-three of them at once. For why? The fairy had told the gamekeeper in a dream, to fill the dead dog full of strychnine; and so he did.

And after a while the birds began to gather at Allfowlsness, in thousands and tens of thousands, blackening all the air; swans and brant geese, harlequins and eiders, harolds and garganeys, smews and goosanders, divers and loons, grebes

and dovekies, auks and razor-bills, gannets and
petrels, skuas and terns, with gulls beyond all
naming or numbering; and they paddled and
washed and splashed and combed and brushed
themselves on the sand, till the shore was white
with feathers; and they quacked and clucked and
gabbled and chattered and screamed and whooped
as they talked over matters with their friends, and
settled where they were to go and breed that
summer, till you might have heard them ten miles
off; and lucky it was for them that there was no
one to hear them but the old keeper, who lived
all alone upon the Ness, in a turf hut thatched
with heather and fringed round with great stones
slung across the roof by bent-ropes, lest the winter
gales should blow the hut right away.   But he
never minded the birds nor hurt them, because
they were not in season; indeed, he minded but
two things in the whole world, and those were,
his Bible and his grouse; for he was as good an
old Scotchman as ever knit stockings on a winter's
night: only, when all the birds were going, he
toddled out, and took off his cap to them, and
wished them a merry journey and a safe return;
and then gathered up all the feathers which they
had left, and cleaned them to sell down south, and
make feather-beds for stuffy people to lie on.

Then the petrels asked this bird and that
whether they would take Tom to Shiny Wall:
but one set was going to Sutherland, and one
to the Shetlands, and one to Norway, and one
to Spitzbergen, and one to Iceland, and one to

Greenland : but none would go to Shiny Wall. So the good-natured petrels said that they would show him part of the way themselves, but they were only going as far as Jan Mayen's Land; and after that he must shift for himself.

And then all the birds rose up, and streamed away in long black lines, north, and north-east, and north-west, across the bright blue summer sky; and their cry was like ten thousand packs of hounds, and ten thousand peals of bells. Only the puffins stayed behind, and killed the young rabbits, and laid their eggs in the rabbit-burrows; which was rough practice, certainly; but a man must see to his own family.

And, as Tom and the petrels went north-eastward, it began to blow right hard; for the old gentleman in the grey great-coat, who looks after the big copper boiler, in the gulf of Mexico, had got behindhand with his work; so Mother Carey had sent an electric message to him for more steam; and now the steam was coming, as much in an hour as ought to have come in a week, puffing and roaring and swishing and swirling, till you could not see where the sky ended and the sea began. But Tom and the petrels never cared, for the gale was right abaft, and away they went over the crests of the billows, as merry as so many flying-fish.

And at last they saw an ugly sight—the black side of a great ship, water-logged in the trough of the sea. Her funnel and her masts were overboard, and swayed and surged under her lee; her decks were swept as clean as a barn floor, and there was no living soul on board.

The petrels flew up to her, and wailed round her; for they were very sorry indeed, and also they expected to find some salt pork; and Tom scrambled on board of her and looked round, frightened and sad.

And there, in a little cot, lashed tight under the bulwark, lay a baby fast asleep; the very same baby, Tom saw at once, which he had seen in the singing lady's arms.

He went up to it, and wanted to wake it; but behold, from under the cot out jumped a little black and tan terrier dog, and began barking and snapping at Tom, and would not let him touch the cot.

Tom knew the dog's teeth could not hurt him: but at least it could shove him away, and did; and he and the dog fought and struggled, for he wanted to help the baby, and did not want to throw the poor dog overboard: but as they were struggling, there came a tall green sea, and walked in over the weather side of the ship, and swept them all into the waves.

"Oh, the baby, the baby!" screamed Tom: but the next moment he did not scream at all; for he saw the cot settling down through the green water, with the baby, smiling in it, fast asleep; and he saw the fairies come up from below, and carry baby and cradle gently down in their soft arms; and then he knew it was all right, and that there would be a new water-baby in St. Brandan's Isle.

And the poor little dog?

Why, after he had kicked and coughed a little, he sneezed so hard, that he sneezed himself clean out of his skin, and turned into a water-dog, and jumped and danced round Tom, and ran over the crests of the waves, and snapped at the jelly-fish and the mackerel, and followed Tom the whole way to the Other-end-of-Nowhere.

Then they went on again, till they began to see the peak of Jan Mayen's Land, standing up like a white sugar-loaf, two miles above the clouds.

And there they fell in with a whole flock of mollymocks, who were feeding on a dead whale.

"These are the fellows to show you the way," said Mother Carey's chickens; "we cannot help you farther north. We don't like to get among the ice pack, for fear it should nip our toes: but the mollys dare fly anywhere."

So the petrels called to the mollys: but they were so busy and greedy, gobbling and pecking and spluttering and fighting over the blubber, that they did not take the least notice.

"Come, come," said the petrels, "you lazy greedy lubbers, this young gentleman is going to Mother Carey, and if you don't attend on him, you won't earn your discharge from her, you know."

"Greedy we are," says a great fat old molly, "but lazy we ain't; and, as for lubbers, we're no more lubbers than you. Let's have a look at the lad."

And he flapped right into Tom's face, and
stared at him in the most impudent way (for the
mollys are audacious fellows, as all whalers know),
and then asked him where he hailed from, and
what land he sighted last.

And, when Tom told him, he seemed pleased,
and said he was a good plucked one to have got
so far.

"Come along, lads," he said to the rest, "and
give this little chap a cast over the pack, for
Mother Carey's sake.  We've eaten blubber
enough for to-day, and we'll e'en work out a
bit of our time by helping the lad."

So the mollys took Tom up on their backs,
and flew off with him, laughing and joking—and
oh, how they did smell of train oil !

"Who are you, you jolly birds?" asked Tom.

"We are the spirits of the old Greenland
skippers (as every sailor knows), who hunted here,
right whales and horse-whales, full hundreds of
years agone.  But, because we were saucy and
greedy, we were all turned into mollys, to eat
whale's blubber all our days.  But lubbers we are
none, and could sail a ship now against any man
in the North seas, though we don't hold with this
new-fangled steam.  And it's a shame of those
black imps of petrels to call us so ; but because
they're her grace's pets, they think they may say
anything they like."

"And who are you?" asked Tom of him, for
he saw that he was the king of all the birds.

"My name is Hendrick Hudson, and a right

215

good skipper was I; and my name will last to the world's end, in spite of all the wrong I did. For I discovered Hudson River, and I named Hudson's Bay; and many have come in my wake that dared not have shown me the way. But I was a hard man in my time, that's truth, and stole the poor Indians off the coast of Maine, and sold them for slaves down in Virginia; and at last I was so cruel to my sailors, here in these very seas, that they set me adrift in an open boat, and I never was heard of more. So now I'm the king of all mollys, till I've worked out my time."

And now they came to the edge of the pack, and beyond it they could see Shiny Wall looming, through mist, and snow, and storm. But the pack rolled horribly upon the swell, and the ice giants fought and roared, and leapt upon each other's backs, and ground each other to powder, so that Tom was afraid to venture among them, lest he should be ground to powder too. And he was the more afraid, when he saw lying among the ice pack the wrecks of many a gallant ship; some with masts and yards all standing, some with the seamen frozen fast on board. Alas, alas, for them! They were all true English hearts; and they came to their end like good knights-errant, in searching for the white gate that never was opened yet.

But the good mollys took Tom and his dog up, and flew with them safe over the pack and the roaring ice giants, and set them down at the foot of Shiny Wall.

"And where is the gate?" asked Tom.

" There is no gate," said the mollys.

" No gate? " cried Tom, aghast.

" None; never a crack of one, and that's the whole of the secret, as better fellows, lad, than you have found to their cost; and if there had been, they'd have killed by now every right whale that swims the sea."

" What am I to do, then? "

" Dive under the floe, to be sure, if you have pluck."

" I've not come so far to turn now," said Tom; " so here goes for a header."

" A lucky voyage to you, lad," said the mollys; " we knew you were one of the right sort. So good-bye."

" Why don't you come too? " asked Tom.

But the mollys only wailed sadly, " We can't go yet, we can't go yet," and flew away over the pack.

So Tom dived under the great white gate which never was opened yet, and went on in black darkness, at the bottom of the sea, for seven days and seven nights. And yet he was not a bit frightened. Why should he be? He was a brave English lad, whose business is to go out and see all the world.

And at last he saw the light, and clear clear water overhead; and up he came a thousand fathoms, among clouds of sea-moths, which fluttered round his head. There were moths with pink heads and wings and opal bodies, that flapped about slowly; moths with brown wings that flapped about quickly; yellow shrimps that hopped and skipped most quickly of all; and jellies of all the colours in the world, that neither hopped nor skipped, but only dawdled and yawned, and would not get out of his way. The dog snapped at them till his jaws were tired; but Tom hardly minded them at all, he was so eager to get to the top of the water, and see the pool where the good whales go.

And a very large pool it was, miles and miles across, though the air was so clear that the ice cliffs on the opposite side looked as if they were close at hand. All round it the ice cliffs rose, in walls and spires and battlements, and caves and bridges, and stories and galleries, in which the ice-fairies live, and drive away the storms and clouds, that Mother Carey's pool may lie calm from year's end to year's end. And the sun acted policeman, and walked round outside every day, peeping just over the top of the ice wall, to see that all went right; and now and then he played conjuring tricks, or had an exhibition of fireworks, to amuse the ice-fairies. For he would make himself into four or five suns at once, or paint the sky with rings and crosses and crescents of white fire, and stick himself in the middle of them, and wink at the fairies; and I daresay they were very much amused; for anything's fun in the country.

And there the good whales lay, the happy sleepy beasts, upon the still oily sea. They were all right whales, you must know, and finners, and razor-backs, and bottle-noses, and spotted sea-

unicorns with long ivory horns.  But the sperm
whales are such raging, ramping, roaring, rum-
bustious fellows, that, if Mother Carey let them
in, there would be no more peace in Peacepool.
So she packs them away in a great pond by themselves at the South Pole, two hundred and sixty-
three miles south-south-east of Mount Erebus, the
great volcano in the ice; and there they butt each
other with their ugly noses, day and night from
year's end to year's end.

But here there were only good quiet beasts,
lying about like the black hulls of sloops, and
blowing every now and then jets of white steam,
or sculling round with their huge mouths open,
for the sea-moths to swim down their throats.
There were no threshers there to thresh their
poor old backs, or sword-fish to stab their
stomachs, or saw-fish to rip them up, or ice-
sharks to bite lumps out of their sides, or whalers
to harpoon and lance them.  They were quite safe
and happy there; and all they had to do was to
wait quietly in Peacepool, till Mother Carey sent
for them to make them out of old beasts into new.

Tom swam up to the nearest whale, and asked
the way to Mother Carey.

"There she sits in the middle," said the whale.

Tom looked; but he could see nothing in the
middle of the pool, but one peaked iceberg: and
he said so.

"That's Mother Carey," said the whale, "as
you will find when you get to her.   There she sits
making old beasts into new all the year round."

" How does she do that ? "

" That's her concern, not mine," said the old whale ; and yawned so wide (for he was very large) that there swam into his mouth 943 sea-moths, 13,846 jelly-fish no bigger than pins' heads, a string of salpæ nine yards long, and forty-three little ice-crabs, who gave each other a parting pinch all round, tucked their legs under their stomachs, and determined to die decently, like Julius Cæsar.

" I suppose," said Tom, " she cuts up a great whale like you into a whole shoal of porpoises ? "

At which the old whale laughed so violently that he coughed up all the creatures ; who swam away again very thankful at having escaped out of that terrible whalebone net of his, from which bourne no traveller returns; and Tom went on to the iceberg, wondering.

And, when he came near it, it took the form of the grandest old lady he had ever seen—a white marble lady, sitting on a white marble throne. And from the foot of the throne there swum away, out and out into the sea, millions of new-born creatures, of more shapes and colours than man ever dreamed. And they were Mother Carey's children, whom she makes out of the sea-water all day long.

He expected, of course — like some grown people who ought to know better—to find her snipping, piecing, fitting, stitching, cobbling, basting, filing, planing, hammering, turning, polishing, moulding, measuring, chiselling, clipping, and so forth, as men do when they go to work to make anything.

But, instead of that, she sat quite still with her chin upon her hand, looking down into the sea with two great grand blue eyes, as blue as the sea itself. Her hair was as white as the snow—for she was very very old—in fact, as old as anything which you are likely to come across, except the difference between right and wrong.

And, when she saw Tom, she looked at him very kindly.

" What do you want, my little man ? It is long since I have seen a water-baby here."

Tom told her his errand, and asked the way to the Other-end-of-Nowhere.

" You ought to know yourself, for you have been there already."

"Have I, ma'am? I'm sure I forget all about it."

"Then look at me."

And, as Tom looked into her great blue eyes, he recollected the way perfectly.

Now, was not that strange ?

"Thank you, ma'am," said Tom. "Then I won't trouble your ladyship any more; I hear you are very busy."

" I am never more busy than I am now," she said, without stirring a finger.

" I heard, ma'am, that you were always making new beasts out of old."

" So people fancy. But I am not going to trouble myself to make things, my little dear. I sit here and make them make themselves."

" You are a clever fairy, indeed," thought Tom.
And he was quite right.

That is a grand trick of good old Mother
Carey's, and a grand answer, which she has had
occasion to make several times to impertinent
people.

There was once, for instance, a fairy who was
so clever that she found out how to make butterflies.  I don't mean sham ones ; no : but real live
ones, which would fly, and eat, and lay eggs, and
do everything that they ought; and she was so
proud of her skill that she went flying straight off
to the North Pole, to boast to Mother Carey how
she could make butterflies.

But Mother Carey laughed.

" Know, silly child," she said, " that any one
can make things, if they will take time and trouble
enough: but it is not every one who, like me, can
make things make themselves."

But people do not yet believe that Mother
Carey is as clever as all that comes to; and they
will not till they, too, go the journey to the Other-
end-of-Nowhere.

" And now, my pretty little man," said Mother
Carey, " you are sure you know the way to the
Other-end-of-Nowhere ?"

Tom thought; and behold, he had forgotten it
utterly.

" That is because you took your eyes off me."

Tom looked at her again, and recollected; and
then looked away, and forgot in an instant.

" But what am I to do, ma'am ?  For I can't

keep looking at you when I am somewhere else."

"You must do without me, as most people have to do, for nine hundred and ninety-nine thousandths of their lives; and look at the dog instead; for he knows the way well enough, and will not forget it. Besides, you may meet some very queer-tempered people there, who will not let you pass without this passport of mine, which you must hang round your neck and take care of; and, of course, as the dog will always go behind you, you must go the whole way backward."

"Backward!" cried Tom. "Then I shall not be able to see my way."

"On the contrary, if you look forward, you will not see a step before you, and be certain to go wrong; but, if you look behind you, and watch carefully whatever you have passed, and especially keep your eye on the dog, who goes by instinct, and therefore can't go wrong, then you will know what is coming next, as plainly as if you saw it in a looking-glass."

Tom was very much astonished: but he obeyed her, for he had learnt always to believe what the fairies told him.

"So it is, my dear child," said Mother Carey; "and I will tell you a story, which will show you that I am perfectly right, as it is my custom to be.

"Once on a time, there were two brothers. One was called Prometheus, because he always looked before him, and boasted that he was wise beforehand. The other was called Epimetheus, because he always looked behind him, and did not boast at all ; but said humbly, like the Irishman, that he had sooner prophesy after the event.

"Well, Prometheus was a very clever fellow, of course, and invented all sorts of wonderful things. But, unfortunately, when they were set to work, to work was just what they would not do: wherefore very little has come of them, and very little is left of them ; and now nobody knows what they were, save a few archæological old gentlemen who scratch in queer corners, and find little there save Ptinum Furem, Blaptem Mortisagam, Acarum Horridum, and Tineam Laciniarum.

"But Epimetheus was a very slow fellow, certainly, and went among men for a clod, and a muff, and a milksop, and a slowcoach, and a bloke, and a boodle, and so forth. And very little he did, for many years: but what he did, he never had to do over again.

"And what happened at last ? There came to the two brothers the most beautiful creature that ever was seen, Pandora by name ; which means, All the gifts of the Gods. But because she had a strange box in her hand, this fanciful, forecasting, suspicious, prudential, theoretical, deductive, prophesying Prometheus, who was always settling what was going to happen, would have nothing to do with pretty Pandora and her box.

"But Epimetheus took her and it, as he took everything that came ; and married her for better for worse, as every man ought, whenever he has even the chance of a good wife. And they opened the box between them, of course, to see what was inside: for, else, of what possible use could it have been to them?

"And out flew all the ills which flesh is heir to; all the children of the four great bogies, Self-will, Ignorance, Fear, and Dirt—for instance:

| | |
|---|---|
| *Measles,* | *Famines,* |
| *Monks,* | *Quacks,* |
| *Scarlatina,* | *Unpaid bills,* |
| *Idols,* | *Tight stays,* |
| *Hooping-coughs,* | *Potatoes,* |
| *Popes,* | *Bad Wine,* |
| *Wars,* | *Despots,* |
| *Peacemongers,* | *Demagogues,* |

*And, worst of all, Naughty Boys and Girls.*

But one thing remained at the bottom of the box, and that was, Hope.

"So Epimetheus got a great deal of trouble, as most men do in this world: but he got the three best things in the world into the bargain—a good wife, and experience, and hope : while Prometheus had just as much trouble, and a great deal more (as you will hear), of his own making ; with nothing beside, save fancies spun out of his own brain, as a spider spins her web out of her stomach.

"And Prometheus kept on looking before him so far ahead, that as he was running about with a box of lucifers (which were the only useful things he ever invented, and do as much harm as good), he trod on his own nose, and tumbled down (as

most deductive philosophers do), whereby he set
the Thames on fire ; and they have hardly put it
out again yet.   So he had to be chained to the top
of a mountain, with a vulture by him to give him
a peck whenever he stirred, lest he should turn the
whole world upside down with his prophecies and
his theories.

"But stupid old Epimetheus went working
and grubbing on, with the help of his wife Pandora,
always looking behind him to see what had
happened, till he really learnt to know now and
then what would happen next; and understood
so well which side his bread was buttered, and
which way the cat jumped, that he began to make
things which would work, and go on working,
too ;  to till and drain the ground, and to make
looms, and ships, and railroads, and steam ploughs,
and electric telegraphs, and all the things which
you see in the Great Exhibition ; and to foretell
famine, and bad weather, and the price of stocks and
(what is hardest of all) the next vagary of the great
idol Whirligig, which some call Public Opinion ;
till at last he grew as rich as a Jew, and as fat as
a farmer, and people thought twice before they
meddled with him, but only once before they
asked him to help them ; for, because he earned
his money well, he could afford to spend it well
likewise.

"And his children are the men of science, who
get good lasting work done in the world; but the
children of Prometheus are the fanatics, and the
theorists, and the bigots, and the bores, and the

noisy windy people, who go telling silly folk what
will happen, instead of looking to see what has
happened already."

Now, was not Mother Carey's a wonderful
story?  And, I am happy to say, Tom believed it
every word.

For so it happened to Tom likewise.  He was
very sorely tried; for though, by keeping the dog
to heels (or rather to toes, for he had to walk backward), he could see pretty well which way the dog
was hunting, yet it was much slower work to go
backwards than to go forwards.  But, what was
more trying still, no sooner had he got out of
Peacepool, than there came running to him all the
conjurers, fortune-tellers, astrologers, prophesiers,
projectors, prestigiators, as many as were in those
parts (and there are too many of them everywhere),
Old Mother Shipton on her broomstick, with
Merlin, Thomas the Rhymer, Gerbertus, Rabanus
Maurus, Nostradamus, Zadkiel, Raphael, Moore,
Old Nixon, and a good many in black coats and
white ties who might have known better, considering in what century they were born, all bawl-
ing and screaming at him, " Look a-head, only look
a-head ; and we will show you what man never
saw before, and right away to the end of the
world ! "

But I am proud to say that, though Tom had
not been to Cambridge—for, if he had, he would
have certainly been senior wrangler—he was such
a little dogged, hard, gnarly, foursquare brick of
an English boy, that he never turned his head

round once all the way from Peacepool to the
Other-end-of-Nowhere : but kept his eye on the
dog, and let him pick out the scent, hot or cold,
straight or crooked, wet or dry, up hill or down
dale ; by which means he never made a single
mistake, and saw all the wonderful and hitherto
by-no-mortal-man-imagined things, which it is my
duty to relate to you in the next chapter.

"Come to me, O ye children !
    For I hear you at your play ;
And the questions that perplexed me
    Have vanished quite away.

" Ye open the Eastern windows,
    That look towards the sun,
Where thoughts are singing swallows,
    And the brooks of morning run.

        *    *    *    *    *

" For what are all our contrivings
    And the wisdom of our books,
When compared with your caresses,
    And the gladness of your looks ?

" Ye are better than all the ballads
    That ever were sung or said ;
For ye are living poems,
    And all the rest are dead."—Longfellow.

and a pumping, as of all the steam-engines in the
world at once. And, when he came near, the
water grew boiling-hot ; not that that hurt him
in the least : but it also grew as foul as gruel ;
and every moment he stumbled over dead shells,
and fish, and sharks, and seals, and whales, which
had been killed by the hot water.

And at last he came to the great sea-serpent
himself, lying dead at the bottom ; and as he was
too thick to scramble over, Tom had to walk
round him three-quarters of a mile and more,
which put him out of his path sadly ; and, when
he had got round, he came to the place called
Stop. And there he stopped, and just in time.

For he was on the edge of a vast hole in the
bottom of the sea, up which was rushing and
roaring clear steam enough to work all the engines
in the world at once ; so clear, indeed, that it was
quite light at moments ; and Tom could see almost
up to the top of the water above, and down below
into the pit for nobody knows how far.

But, as soon as he bent his head over the edge,
he got such a rap on the nose from pebbles, that he
jumped back again ; for the steam, as it rushed up,
rasped away the sides of the hole, and hurled it up
into the sea in a shower of mud and gravel and
ashes ; and then it spread all around, and sank
again, and covered in the dead fish so fast, that
before Tom had stood there five minutes he was
buried in silt up to his ankles, and began to be
afraid that he should have been buried alive.

And perhaps he would have been, but that

while he was thinking, the whole piece of ground on which he stood was torn off and blown upwards, and away flew Tom a mile up through the sea, wondering what was coming next.

At last he stopped—thump! and found himself tight in the legs of the most wonderful bogy which he had ever seen.

It had I don't know how many wings, as big as the sails of a windmill, and spread out in a ring like them; and with them it hovered over the steam which rushed up, as a ball hovers over the top of a fountain. And for every wing above it had a leg below, with a claw like a comb at the tip, and a nostril at the root; and in the middle it had no stomach and one eye; and as for its mouth, that was all on one side, as the madreporiform tubercle in a star-fish is. Well, it was a very strange beast; but no stranger than some dozens which you may see.

"What do you want here," it cried quite peevishly, "getting in my way?" and it tried to drop Tom : but he held on tight to its claws, thinking himself safer where he was.

So Tom told him who he was, and what his errand was. And the thing winked its one eye, and sneered :

"I am too old to be taken in in that way. You are come after gold—I know you are."

"Gold! What is gold?" And really Tom did not know ; but the suspicious old bogy would not believe him.

But after a while Tom began to understand a

little.   For, as the vapours came up out of the hole, the bogy smelt them with his nostrils, and combed them and sorted them with his combs ; and then, when they steamed up through them against his wings, they were changed into showers and streams of metal.   From one wing fell gold-dust, and from another silver, and from another copper, and from another tin, and from another lead, and so on, and sank into the soft mud, into veins and cracks, and hardened there.   Whereby it comes to pass that the rocks are full of metal.

But, all of a sudden, somebody shut off the steam below, and the hole was left empty in an instant : and then down rushed the water into the hole, in such a whirlpool that the bogy spun round and round as fast as a teetotum.   But that was all in his day's work, like a fair fall with the hounds ; so all he did was to say to Tom—

"Now is your time, youngster, to get down, if you are in earnest, which I don't believe."

"You'll soon see," said Tom ; and away he went, as bold as Baron Munchausen, and shot down the rushing cataract like a salmon at Ballisodare.

And, when he got to the bottom, he swam till he was washed on shore safe upon the Other-end-of-Nowhere ; and he found it, to his surprise, as most other people do, much more like This-End-of-Somewhere than he had been in the habit of expecting.

And first he went through Waste-paper-land, where all the stupid books lie in heaps, up hill and

down dale, like leaves in a winter wood ; and there
he saw people digging and grubbing among them,
to make worse books out of bad ones, and thrashing chaff to save the dust of it ; and a very
good trade they drove thereby, especially among
children.

Then he went by the sea of slops, to the mountain of messes, and the territory of tuck, where the
ground was very sticky, for it was all made of bad
toffee (not Everton toffee, of course), and full of
deep cracks and holes choked with wind-fallen
fruit, and green gooseberries, and sloes, and crabs,
and whinberries, and hips and haws, and all the
nasty things which little children will eat, if they
can get them.   But the fairies hide them out of the
way in that country as fast as they can, and very
hard work they have, and of very little use it is.
For as fast as they hide away the old trash, foolish
and wicked people make fresh trash full of lime
and poisonous paints, and actually go and steal
receipts out of old Madame Science's big book to
invent poisons for little children, and sell them at
wakes and fairs and tuck-shops.   Very well.   Let
them go on.   Dr. Letheby and Dr. Hassall cannot
catch them, though they are setting traps for them
all day long.   But the Fairy with the birch-rod
will catch them all in time, and make them begin
at one corner of their shops, and eat their way out
at the other : by which time they will have got
such stomach-aches as will cure them of poisoning
little children.

Next he saw all the little people in the world,

writing all the little books in the world, about all
the other little people in the world ; probably
because they had no great people to write about :
and if the names of the books were not Squeeky,
nor the Pump-lighter, nor the Narrow Narrow
World, nor the Hills of the Chattermuch, nor the
Children's Twaddeday, why then they were something else.   And all the rest of the little people in
the world read the books, and thought themselves
each as good as the President ; and perhaps they
were right, for every one knows his own business
best.   But Tom thought he would sooner have a
jolly good fairy tale, about Jack the Giant-killer
or Beauty and the Beast, which taught him something that he didn't know already.

And next he came to the centre of Creation
(the hub, they call it there), which lies in latitude
42.21° south, and longitude 108.56° east.

And there he found all the wise people instruct-
ing mankind in the science of spirit-rapping, while
their house was burning over their heads : and
when Tom told them of the fire, they held an
indignation meeting forthwith, and unanimously
determined to hang Tom's dog for coming into
their country with gunpowder in his mouth.   Tom
couldn't help saying that though they did fancy
they had carried all the wit away with them out of
Lincolnshire two hundred years ago, yet if they had
had one such Lincolnshire nobleman among them
as good old Lord Yarborough, he would have called
for the fire-engines before he hanged other people's
dogs.   But it was of no use, and the dog was

hanged: and Tom couldn't even have his carcase; for they had abolished the have-his-carcase act in that country, for fear lest when rogues fell out, honest men should come by their own.   And so they would have succeeded perfectly, as they always do, only that (as they also always do) they failed in one little particular, viz. that the dog would not die, being a water-dog, but bit their fingers so abominably that they were forced to let him go, and Tom likewise, as British subjects.   Whereon they recommenced rapping for the spirits of their fathers ; and very much astonished the poor old spirits were when they came, and saw how, according to the laws of Mrs. Bedonebyasyoudid, their descendants had weakened their constitution by hard living.

Then came Tom to the Island of Polupragmosyne (which some call Rogues' Harbour; but they are wrong ; for that is in the middle of Bramshill Bushes, and the county police have cleared it out long ago).   There every one knows his neighbour's business better than his own ; and a very noisy place it is, as might be expected, considering that all the inhabitants are *ex officio* on the wrong side of the house in the " Parliament of Man, and the Federation of the World " ; and are always making wry mouths, and crying that the fairies' grapes were sour.

There Tom saw ploughs drawing horses, nails driving hammers, birds' nests taking boys, books making authors, bulls keeping china - shops, monkeys shaving cats, dead dogs drilling live lions, blind brigadiers shelfed as principals of colleges, play-actors not in the least shelfed as popular preachers; and, in short, every one set to do something which he had not learnt, because in what he had learnt, or pretended to learn, he had failed.

There stands the Pantheon of the Great Unsuccessful, from the builders of the Tower of Babel to those of the Trafalgar Fountains; in which politicians lecture on the constitutions which ought to have marched, conspirators on the revolutions which ought to have succeeded, economists on the schemes which ought to have made every one's fortune, and projectors on the discoveries which ought to have set the Thames on fire. There cobblers lecture on orthopedy (whatsoever that may be) because they cannot sell their shoes; and poets on Æsthetics (whatsoever that may be) because they cannot sell their poetry. There philosophers demonstrate that England would be the freest and richest country in the world, if she would only turn Papist again; penny-a-liners abuse the *Times*, because they have not wit enough to get on its staff; and young ladies walk about with lockets of Charles the First's hair (or of somebody else's, when the Jews' genuine stock is used up), inscribed with the neat and appropriate legend—which indeed is popular through all that land, and which, I hope, you will learn to translate in due time and to perpend likewise:—

"*Victrix causa diis placuit, sed victa puellis.*"

When he got into the middle of the town, they

all set on him at once, to show him his way; or rather, to show him that he did not know his way; for as for asking him what way he wanted to go, no one ever thought of that.

But one pulled him hither, and another poked him thither, and a third cried—

"You mustn't go west, I tell you; it is destruction to go west."

"But I am not going west, as you may see," said Tom.

And another, "The east lies here, my dear; I assure you this is the east."

"But I don't want to go east," said Tom.

"Well, then, at all events, whichever way you are going, you are going wrong," cried they all with one voice—which was the only thing which they ever agreed about; and all pointed at once to all the thirty-and-two points of the compass, till Tom thought all the sign-posts in England had got together, and fallen fighting.

And whether he would have ever escaped out of the town, it is hard to say, if the dog had not taken it into his head that they were going to pull his master in pieces, and tackled them so sharply about the gastrocnemius muscle, that he gave them some business of their own to think of at last; and while they were rubbing their bitten calves, Tom and the dog got safe away.

On the borders of that island he found Gotham, where the wise men live; the same who dragged the pond because the moon had fallen into it, and planted a hedge round the cuckoo, to keep spring all the year. And he found them bricking up the town gate, because it was so wide that little folks could not get through. And, when he asked why, they told him they were expanding their liturgy. So he went on; for it was no business of his: only he could not help saying that in his country, if the kitten could not get in at the same hole as the cat, she might stay outside and mew.

But he saw the end of such fellows, when he came to the island of the Golden Asses, where nothing but thistles grow. For there they were all turned into mokes with ears a yard long, for meddling with matters which they do not understand, as Lucius did in the story. And like him, mokes they must remain, till, by the laws of development, the thistles develop into roses. Till then, they must comfort themselves with the thought, that the longer their ears are, the thicker their hides; and so a good beating don't hurt them.

Then came Tom to the great land of Hearsay, in which are no less than thirty and odd kings, beside half a dozen Republics, and perhaps more by next mail.

And there he fell in with a deep, dark, deadly, and destructive war, waged by the princes and potentates of those parts, both spiritual and temporal, against what do you think? One thing I am sure of. That unless I told you, you would never know; nor how they waged that war either; for all their strategy and art military consisted in the safe and easy process of stopping their ears and screaming, "Oh, don't tell us!" and then running away.

So when Tom came into that land, he found them all, high and low, man, woman, and child, running for their lives day and night continually, and entreating not to be told they didn't know what : only the land being an island, and they having a dislike to the water (being a musty lot for the most part), they ran round and round the shore for ever, which (as the island was exactly of the same circumference as the planet on which we have the honour of living) was hard work, especially to those who had business to look after.   But before them, as bandmaster and fugleman, ran a gentleman shearing a pig; the melodious strains of which animal led them for ever, if not to conquest, still to flight; and kept up their spirits mightily with the thought that they would at least have the pig's wool for their pains.

And running after them, day and night, came such a poor, lean, seedy, hard-worked old giant, as ought to have been cockered up, and had a good dinner given him, and a good wife found him, and been set to play with little children; and then he would have been a very presentable old fellow after all; for he had a heart, though it was considerably overgrown with brains.

He was made up principally of fish bones and parchment, put together with wire and Canada balsam; and smelt strongly of spirits, though he never drank anything but water: but spirits he used somehow, there was no denying.  He had a great pair of spectacles on his nose, and a butterfly-net in one hand, and a geological hammer in the other; and was hung all over with pockets, full of collecting boxes, bottles, microscopes, telescopes, barometers, ordnance maps, scalpels, forceps, photographic apparatus, and all other tackle for finding out everything about everything, and a little more too. And, most strange of all, he was running not forwards but backwards, as fast as he could.

Away all the good folks ran from him, except Tom, who stood his ground and dodged between his legs; and the giant, when he had passed him, looked down, and cried, as if he was quite pleased and comforted,—

"What? who are you? And you actually don't run away, like all the rest?" But he had to take his spectacles off, Tom remarked, in order to see him plainly.

Tom told him who he was; and the giant pulled out a bottle and a cork instantly, to collect him with.

But Tom was too sharp for that, and dodged between his legs and in front of him; and then the giant could not see him at all.

"No, no, no!" said Tom, "I've not been round the world, and through the world, and up to Mother Carey's haven, beside being caught in a net and called a Holothurian and a Cephalopod, to be bottled up by any old giant like you."

And when the giant understood what a great traveller Tom had been, he made a truce with him at once, and would have kept him there to this day to pick his brains, so delighted was he at finding any one to tell him what he did not know before.

"Ah, you lucky little dog!" said he at last, quite simply—for he was the simplest, pleasantest, honestest, kindliest old Dominie Sampson of a giant that ever turned the world upside down without intending it—"ah, you lucky little dog! If I had only been where you have been, to see what you have seen!"

"Well," said Tom, "if you want to do that, you had best put your head under water for a few hours, as I did, and turn into a water-baby, or some other baby, and then you might have a chance."

"Turn into a baby, eh? If I could do that, and know what was happening to me for but one hour, I should know everything then, and be at rest. But I can't; I can't be a little child again; and I suppose if I could, it would be no use, because then I should know nothing about what was happening to me. Ah, you lucky little dog!" said the poor old giant.

"But why do you run after all these poor people?" said Tom, who liked the giant very much.

"My dear, it's they that have been running after me, father and son, for hundreds and hundreds of years, throwing stones at me till they have knocked off my spectacles fifty times, and calling me a malignant and a turbaned Turk, who beat a Venetian and traduced the State—goodness only knows what they mean, for I never read poetry—

and hunting me round and round—though catch me they can't, for every time I go over the same ground, I go the faster, and grow the bigger. While all I want is to be friends with them, and to tell them something to their advantage, like Mr. Joseph Ady: only somehow they are so strangely afraid of hearing it. But, I suppose I am not a man of the world, and have no tact."

"But why don't you turn round and tell them so?"

"Because I can't. You see, I am one of the sons of Epimetheus, and must go backwards, if I am to go at all."

"But why don't you stop, and let them come up to you?"

"Why, my dear, only think. If I did, all the butterflies and cockyolybirds would fly past me, and then I should catch no more new species, and should grow rusty and mouldy, and die. And I don't intend to do that, my dear; for I have a destiny before me, they say: though what it is I don't know, and don't care."

"Don't care?" said Tom.

"No. Do the duty which lies nearest you, and catch the first beetle you come across, is my motto; and I have thriven by it for some hundred years. Now I must go on. Dear me, while I have been talking to you, at least nine new species have escaped me."

And on went the giant, behind before, like a bull in a china-shop, till he ran into the steeple of the great idol temple (for they are all idolaters in those parts, of course, else they would never be afraid of giants), and knocked the upper half clean off, hurting himself horribly about the small of the back.

But little he cared; for as soon as the ruins of the steeple were well between his legs, he poked and peered among the falling stones, and shifted his spectacles, and pulled out his pocket-magnifier, and cried—

"An entirely new Oniscus, and three obscure Podurellæ! Besides a moth which M. le Roi des Papillons (though he, like all Frenchmen, is given to hasty inductions) says is confined to the limits of the Glacial Drift. This is most important!"

And down he sat on the nave of the temple (not being a man of the world) to examine his Podurellæ. Whereon (as was to be expected) the roof caved in bodily, smashing the idols, and sending the priests flying out of doors and windows, like rabbits out of a burrow when a ferret goes in.

But he never heeded; for out of the dust flew a bat, and the giant had him in a moment.

"Dear me! This is even more important! Here is a cognate species to that which Macgilliwaukie Brown insists is confined to the Buddhist temples of Little Thibet; and now when I look at it, it may be only a variety produced by difference of climate!"

And having bagged his bat, up he got, and on he went; while all the people ran, being in none the better humour for having their temple smashed for the sake of three obscure species of Podurella, and a Buddhist bat.

"Well," thought Tom, "this is a very pretty quarrel, with a good deal to be said on both sides. But it is no business of mine."

And no more it was, because he was a water-baby, and had the original sow by the right ear; which you will never have, unless you be a baby, whether of the water, the land, or the air, matters not, provided you can only keep on continually being a baby.

So the giant ran round after the people, and the people ran round after the giant, and they are running unto this day for aught I know, or do not know; and will run till either he, or they, or both, turn into little children.   And then, as Shakespeare says (and therefore it must be true)—

"*Jack shall have Gill*
*Nought shall go ill*
*The man shall have his mare again, and all go well.*"

Then Tom came to a very famous island, which was called, in the days of the great traveller Captain Gulliver, the Isle of Laputa.   But Mrs. Bedonebyasyoudid has named it over again the Isle of Tomtoddies, all heads and no bodies.

And when Tom came near it, he heard such a grumbling and grunting and growling and wailing and weeping and whining that he thought people must be ringing little pigs, or cropping puppies' ears, or drowning kittens: but when he came nearer still, he began to hear words among the noise; which was the Tomtoddies' song which they sing morning and evening, and all night too, to their great idol Examination—

"*I can't learn my lesson: the examiner's coming !*"

And that was the only song which they knew.

And when Tom got on shore the first thing he saw was a great pillar, on one side of which was inscribed, "Playthings not allowed here"; at which he was so shocked that he would not stay to see what was written on the other side. Then he looked round for the people of the island : but instead of men, women, and children, he found nothing but turnips and radishes, beet and mangold wurzel, without a single green leaf among them, and half of them burst and decayed, with toad-stools growing out of them. Those which were left began crying to Tom, in half a dozen different languages at once, and all of them badly spoken, "I can't learn my lesson; do come and help me!" And one cried, "Can you show me how to extract this square root?"

And another, "Can you tell me the distance between α Lyræ and β Camelopardis?"

And another, "What is the latitude and longitude of Snooksville, in Noman's County, Oregon, U.S.?"

And another, "What was the name of Mutius Scævola's thirteenth cousin's grandmother's maid's cat?"

And another, "How long would it take a school-inspector of average activity to tumble head over heels from London to York?"

And another, "Can you tell me the name of a place that nobody ever heard of, where nothing ever happened, in a country which has not been discovered yet?"

And another, "Can you show me how to correct this hopelessly corrupt passage of Graidio-colosyrtus Tabenniticus, on the cause why crocodiles have no tongues?"

And so on, and so on, and so on, till one would have thought they were all trying for tide-waiters' places, or cornetcies in the heavy dragoons.

"And what good on earth will it do you if I did tell you?" quoth Tom.

Well, they didn't know that: all they knew was the examiner was coming.

Then Tom stumbled on the hugest and softest nimblecomequick turnip you ever saw filling a hole in a crop of swedes, and it cried to him, "Can you tell me anything at all about anything you like?"

"About what?" says Tom.

"About anything you like; for as fast as I learn things I forget them again. So my mamma says that my intellect is not adapted for methodic science, and says that I must go in for general information."

Tom told him that he did not know general information, nor any officers in the army; only he had a friend once that went for a drummer: but he could tell him a great many strange things which he had seen in his travels.

So he told him prettily enough, while the poor turnip listened very carefully; and the more he listened, the more he forgot, and the more water ran out of him.

Tom thought he was crying: but it was only his poor brains running away, from being worked so hard; and as Tom talked, the unhappy turnip streamed down all over with juice, and split and shrank till nothing was left of him but rind and water; whereat Tom ran away in a fright, for he thought he might be taken up for killing the turnip.

But, on the contrary, the turnip's parents were highly delighted, and considered him a saint and a martyr, and put up a long inscription over his tomb about his wonderful talents, early development, and unparalleled precocity.  Were they not a foolish couple?  But there was a still more foolish couple next to them, who were beating a wretched little radish, no bigger than my thumb, for sullenness and obstinacy and wilful stupidity, and never knew that the reason why it couldn't learn or hardly even speak was, that there was a great worm inside it eating out all its brains.  But even they are no foolisher than some hundred score of papas and mammas, who fetch the rod when they ought to fetch a new toy, and send to the dark cupboard instead of to the doctor.

Tom was so puzzled and frightened with all he saw, that he was longing to ask the meaning of it;

and at last he stumbled over a respectable old stick lying half covered with earth. But a very stout and worthy stick it was, for it belonged to good Roger Ascham in old time, and had carved on its head King Edward the Sixth, with the Bible in his hand.

"You see," said the stick, "there were as pretty little children once as you could wish to see, and might have been so still if they had been only left to grow up like human beings, and then handed over to me; but their foolish fathers and mothers, instead of letting them pick flowers, and make dirt-pies, and get birds' nests, and dance round the gooseberry bush, as little children should, kept them always at lessons, working, working, working, learning week-day lessons all week-days, and Sunday lessons all Sunday, and weekly examinations every Saturday, and monthly examinations every month, and yearly examinations every year, everything seven times over, as if once was not enough, and enough as good as a feast—till their brains grew big, and their bodies grew small, and they were all changed into turnips, with little but water inside; and still their foolish parents actually pick the leaves off them as fast as they grow, lest they should have anything green about them."

"Ah!" said Tom, "if dear Mrs. Doasyou-wouldbedoneby knew of it she would send them a lot of tops, and balls, and marbles, and ninepins, and make them all as jolly as sand-boys."

"It would be no use," said the stick. "They can't play now, if they tried. Don't you see how their legs have turned to roots and grown into the ground, by never taking any exercise, but sapping and moping always in the same place ?  But here comes the Examiner-of-all-Examiners.  So you had better get away, I warn you, or he will examine you and your dog into the bargain, and set him to examine all the other dogs, and you to examine all the other water-babies.  There is no escaping out of his hands, for his nose is nine thousand miles long, and can go down chimneys, and through keyholes, upstairs, downstairs, in my lady's chamber, examining all little boys, and the little boys' tutors likewise.  But when he is thrashed—so Mrs. Bedonebyasyoudid has promised me—I shall have the thrashing of him : and if I don't lay it on with a will it's a pity."

Tom went off : but rather slowly and surlily ; for he was somewhat minded to face this same Examiner-of-all-Examiners, who came striding among the poor turnips, binding heavy burdens and grievous to be borne, and laying them on little children's shoulders, like the Scribes and Pharisees of old, and not touching the same with one of his fingers ; for he had plenty of money, and a fine house to live in, and so forth ; which was more than the poor little turnips had.

But when he got near, he looked so big and burly and dictatorial, and shouted so loud to Tom, to come and be examined, that Tom ran for his life, and the dog too.  And really it was time ; for the poor turnips, in their hurry and fright, crammed themselves so fast to be ready for the Examiner, that they burst and popped by dozens all round him, till the place sounded like Aldershot on a field-day, and Tom thought he should be blown into the air, dog and all.

As he went down to the shore he passed the poor turnip's new tomb. But Mrs. Bedonebyas-youdid had taken away the epitaph about talents and precocity and development, and put up one of her own instead which Tom thought much more sensible :—

> *" Instruction sore long time I bore,*
> *And cramming was in vain;*
> *Till heaven did please my woes to ease*
> *With water on the brain."*

So Tom jumped into the sea, and swam on his way, singing :—

> *" Farewell, Tomtoddies all; I thank my stars*
> *That nought I know save those three royal r's :*
> *Reading and riting sure, with rithmetick,*
> *Will help a lad of sense through thin and thick."*

Whereby you may see that Tom was no poet : but no more was John Bunyan, though he was as wise a man as you will meet in a month of Sundays.

And next he came to Oldwivesfabledom, where the folks were all heathens, and worshipped a howling ape.

And there he found a little boy sitting in the middle of the road, and crying bitterly.

" What are you crying for ?" said Tom.

" Because I am not as frightened as I could wish to be."

" Not frightened?   You are a queer little chap : but, if you want to be frightened, here goes —Boo !"

" Ah," said the little boy, " that is very kind of you; but I don't feel that it has made any impression."

Tom offered to upset him, punch him, stamp on him, fettle him over the head with a brick, or anything else whatsoever which would give him the slightest comfort.

But he only thanked Tom very civilly, in fine long words which he had heard other folk use, and which, therefore, he thought were fit and proper to use himself; and cried on till his papa and mamma came, and sent off for the Powwow man immediately.   And a very good-natured gentleman and lady they were, though they were heathens; and talked quite pleasantly to Tom about his travels, till the Powwow man arrived, with his thunderbox under his arm.

And a well-fed, ill-favoured gentleman he was, as ever served Her Majesty at Portland.   Tom was a little frightened at first; for he thought it was Grimes.   But he soon saw his mistake : for Grimes always looked a man in the face; and this fellow never did.   And when he spoke, it was fire and smoke; and when he sneezed, it was squibs and crackers; and when he cried (which he did when-ever it paid him), it was boiling pitch; and some of it was sure to stick.

" Here we are again ! " cried he, like the clown in a pantomime. " So you can't feel frightened, my little dear—eh ? I'll do that for you. I'll make an impression on you ! Yah ! Boo ! Whirroo ! Hullabaloo ! "

And he rattled, thumped, brandished his thunderbox, yelled, shouted, raved, roared, stamped, and danced corrobory like any black fellow ; and then he touched a spring in the thunderbox, and out popped turnip-ghosts and magic-lanthorns and pasteboard bogies and spring-heeled Jacks, and sallaballas, with such a horrid din, clatter, clank, roll, rattle, and roar, that the little boy turned up the whites of his eyes, and fainted right away.

And at that his poor heathen papa and mamma were as much delighted as if they had found a gold mine ; and fell down upon their knees before the Powwow man, and gave him a palanquin with a pole of solid silver and curtains of cloth of gold ; and carried him about in it on their own backs : but as soon as they had taken him up, the pole stuck to their shoulders, and they could not set him down any more, but carried him on willynilly, as Sinbad carried the old man of the sea : which was a pitiable sight to see ; for the father was a very brave officer, and wore two swords and a blue button ; and the mother was as pretty a lady as ever had pinched feet like a Chinese. But you see, they had chosen to do a foolish thing just once too often ; so, by the laws of Mrs. Bedonebyasyoudid, they had to go on doing it whether they chose or not, till the coming of the Cocqcigrues.

Ah! don't you wish that some one would go and convert those poor heathens, and teach them not to frighten their little children into fits?

" Now, then," said the Powwow man to Tom, "wouldn't you like to be frightened, my little dear? For I can see plainly that you are a very wicked, naughty, graceless, reprobate boy."

" You're another," quoth Tom, very sturdily. And when the man ran at him, and cried " Boo!" Tom ran at him in return, and cried " Boo!" likewise, right in his face, and set the little dog upon him; and at his legs the dog went.

At which, if you will believe it, the fellow turned tail, thunderbox and all, with a " Woof!" like an old sow on the common; and ran for his life, screaming, " Help! thieves! murder! fire! He is going to kill me! I am a ruined man! He will murder me; and break, burn, and destroy my precious and invaluable thunderbox; and then you will have no more thunder-showers in the land. Help! help! help!"

At which the papa and mamma and all the people of Oldwivesfabledom flew at Tom, shouting, " Oh, the wicked, impudent, hard-hearted, graceless boy! Beat him, kick him, shoot him, drown him, hang him, burn him!" and so forth: but luckily they had nothing to shoot, hang, or burn him with, for the fairies had hid all the killing-tackle out of the way a little while before; so they could only pelt him with stones; and some of the stones went clean through him, and came out the other side. But he did not mind that a bit; for the holes closed up again as fast as they were made, because he was a water-baby. However, he was very glad when he was safe out of the country, for the noise there made him all but deaf.

Then he came to a very quiet place, called Leaveheavenalone. And there the sun was drawing water out of the sea to make steam-threads, and the wind was twisting them up to make cloud-patterns, till they had worked between them the loveliest wedding veil of Chantilly lace, and hung it up in their own Crystal Palace for any one to buy who could afford it; while the good old sea never grudged, for she knew they would pay her back honestly. So the sun span, and the wind wove, and all went well with the great steam-loom; as is likely, considering—and considering—and considering—

And at last, after innumerable adventures, each more wonderful than the last, he saw before him a huge building, much bigger, and—what is most surprising — a little uglier than a certain new lunatic asylum, but not built quite of the same materials. None of it, at least—or, indeed, for aught that I ever saw, any part of any other building whatsoever—is cased with nine-inch brick inside and out, and filled up with rubble between the walls, in order that any gentleman who has been confined during Her Majesty's pleasure may be unconfined during his own pleasure, and take a walk in the neighbouring park to improve his spirits, after an hour's light and wholesome labour with his dinner-fork or one of the legs of his iron bedstead.   No.   The walls of this building were built on an entirely different principle, which need not be described, as it has not yet been discovered.

Tom walked towards this great building, wondering what it was, and having a strange fancy that he might find Mr. Grimes inside it, till he saw running toward him, and shouting " Stop ! " three or four people, who, when they came nearer, were nothing else than policemen's truncheons, running along without legs or arms.

Tom was not astonished.   He was long past that.   Besides, he had seen the naviculæ in the water move nobody knows how, a hundred times, without arms, or legs, or anything to stand in their stead.   Neither was he frightened; for he had been doing no harm.

So he stopped ; and, when the foremost truncheon came up and asked his business, he showed Mother Carey's pass; and the truncheon looked at it in the oddest fashion; for he had one eye in the middle of his upper end, so that when he looked at anything, being quite stiff, he had to slope himself, and poke himself, till it was a wonder why he did not tumble over; but, being quite full of the spirit of justice (as all policemen, and their truncheons, ought to be), he was always in a position of stable equilibrium, whichever way he put himself.

" All right—pass on," said he at last.   And

then he added: " I had better go with you, young man." And Tom had no objection, for such company was both respectable and safe; so the truncheon coiled its thong neatly round its handle, to prevent tripping itself up—for the thong had got loose in running—and marched on by Tom's side.

" Why have you no policeman to carry you ? " asked Tom, after a while.

" Because we are not like those clumsy-made truncheons in the land-world, which cannot go without having a whole man to carry them about. We do our own work for ourselves; and do it very well, though I say it who should not."

" Then why have you a thong to your handle?" asked Tom.

" To hang ourselves up by, of course, when we are off duty."

Tom had got his answer, and had no more to say, till they came up to the great iron door of the prison.   And there the truncheon knocked twice, with its own head.

A wicket in the door opened, and out looked a tremendous old brass blunderbuss charged up to the muzzle with slugs, who was the porter; and Tom started back a little at the sight of him.

" What case is this ? " he asked in a deep voice, out of his broad bell mouth.

" If you please, sir, it is no case; only a young gentleman from her ladyship, who wants to see Grimes, the master-sweep."

" Grimes ? " said the blunderbuss.   And he

pulled in his muzzle, perhaps to look over his
prison-lists.

"Grimes is up chimney No. 345," he said from
inside. "So the young gentleman had better go
on to the roof."

Tom looked up at the enormous wall, which
seemed at least ninety miles high, and wondered
how he should ever get up: but, when he hinted
that to the truncheon, it settled the matter in a
moment. For it whisked round, and gave him
such a shove behind as sent him up to the roof in
no time, with his little dog under his arm.

And there he walked along the leads, till he
met another truncheon, and told him his errand.

"Very good," it said. "Come along : but it
will be of no use. He is the most unremorseful,
hard-hearted, foul-mouthed fellow I have in charge ;
and thinks about nothing but beer and pipes,
which are not allowed here, of course."

So they walked along over the leads, and very
sooty they were, and Tom thought the chimneys
must want sweeping very much. But he was
surprised to see that the soot did not stick to his
feet, or dirty them in the least. Neither did the
live coals, which were lying about in plenty, burn
him; for, being a water-baby, his radical humours
were of a moist and cold nature, as you may read
at large in Lemnius, Cardan, Van Helmont, and
other gentlemen, who knew as much as they could,
and no man can know more.

And at last they came to chimney No. 345.
Out of the top of it, his head and shoulders just

showing, stuck poor Mr. Grimes, so sooty, and bleared, and ugly, that Tom could hardly bear to look at him. And in his mouth was a pipe; but it was not a-light; though he was pulling at it with all his might.

"Attention, Mr. Grimes," said the truncheon; "here is a gentleman come to see you."

But Mr. Grimes only said bad words; and kept grumbling, "My pipe won't draw. My pipe won't draw."

"Keep a civil tongue, and attend!" said the truncheon; and popped up just like Punch, hitting Grimes such a crack over the head with itself, that his brains rattled inside like a dried walnut in its shell. He tried to get his hands out, and rub the place: but he could not, for they were stuck fast in the chimney. Now he was forced to attend.

"Hey!" he said, "why, it's Tom! I suppose you have come here to laugh at me, you spiteful little atomy?"

Tom assured him he had not, but only wanted to help him.

"I don't want anything except beer, and that I can't get; and a light to this bothering pipe, and that I can't get either."

"I'll get you one," said Tom; and he took up a live coal (there were plenty lying about) and put it to Grimes' pipe: but it went out instantly.

"It's no use," said the truncheon, leaning itself up against the chimney and looking on. "I tell you, it is no use. His heart is so cold that it

freezes everything that comes near him. You will
see that presently, plain enough."

"Oh, of course, it's my fault. Everything's
always my fault," said Grimes. "Now don't go
to hit me again" (for the truncheon started upright,
and looked very wicked); "you know, if my arms
were only free, you daren't hit me then."

The truncheon leant back against the chimney,
and took no notice of the personal insult, like a
well-trained policeman as it was, though he was
ready enough to avenge any transgression against
morality or order.

"But can't I help you in any other way?
Can't I help you to get out of this chimney?"
said Tom.

"No," interposed the truncheon; "he has come
to the place where everybody must help themselves; and he will find it out, I hope, before he
has done with me."

"Oh, yes," said Grimes, "of course it's me.
Did I ask to be brought here into the prison? Did
I ask to be set to sweep your foul chimneys? Did
I ask to have lighted straw put under me to make
me go up? Did I ask to stick fast in the very first
chimney of all, because it was so shamefully clogged
up with soot? Did I ask to stay here—I don't
know how long—a hundred years, I do believe,
and never get my pipe, nor my beer, nor nothing
fit for a beast, let alone a man?"

"No," answered a solemn voice behind. "No
more did Tom, when you behaved to him in the
very same way."

It was Mrs. Bedonebyasyoudid. And, when the truncheon saw her, it started bolt upright—Attention!—and made such a low bow, that if it had not been full of the spirit of justice, it must have tumbled on its end, and probably hurt its one eye. And Tom made his bow too.

"Oh, ma'am," he said, "don't think about me; that's all past and gone, and good times and bad times and all times pass over. But may not I help poor Mr. Grimes? Mayn't I try and get some of these bricks away, that he may move his arms?"

"You may try, of course," she said.

So Tom pulled and tugged at the bricks: but he could not move one. And then he tried to wipe Mr. Grimes' face: but the soot would not come off.

"Oh, dear!" he said. "I have come all this way, through all these terrible places, to help you, and now I am of no use at all."

"You had best leave me alone," said Grimes; "you are a good-natured forgiving little chap, and that's truth; but you'd best be off. The hail's coming on soon, and it will beat the eyes out of your little head."

"What hail?"

"Why, hail that falls every evening here; and, till it comes close to me, it's like so much warm rain: but then it turns to hail over my head, and knocks me about like small shot."

"That hail will never come any more," said the strange lady. "I have told you before what it

262

was. It was your mother's tears, those which she shed when she prayed for you by her bedside; but your cold heart froze it into hail. But she is gone to heaven now, and will weep no more for her graceless son."

Then Grimes was silent awhile; and then he looked very sad.

"So my old mother's gone, and I never there to speak to her! Ah! a good woman she was, and might have been a happy one, in her little school there in Vendale, if it hadn't been for me and my bad ways."

"Did she keep the school in Vendale?" asked Tom. And then he told Grimes all the story of his going to her house, and how she could not abide the sight of a chimney-sweep, and then how kind she was, and how he turned into a water-baby.

"Ah!" said Grimes, "good reason she had to hate the sight of a chimney-sweep. I ran away from her and took up with the sweeps, and never let her know where I was, nor sent her a penny to help her, and now it's too late—too late!" said Mr. Grimes.

And he began crying and blubbering like a great baby, till his pipe dropped out of his mouth, and broke all to bits.

"Oh, dear, if I was but a little chap in Vendale again, to see the clear beck, and the apple-orchard, and the yew-hedge, how different I would go on! But it's too late now. So you go along, you kind little chap, and don't stand to look at a man crying,

263

that's old enough to be your father, and never feared the face of man, nor of worse neither. But I'm beat now, and beat I must be. I've made my bed, and I must lie on it. Foul I would be, and foul I am, as an Irishwoman said to me once; and little I heeded it. It's all my own fault: but it's too late." And he cried so bitterly that Tom began crying too.

"Never too late," said the fairy, in such a strange soft new voice that Tom looked up at her; and she was so beautiful for the moment, that Tom half fancied she was her sister.

No more was it too late. For, as poor Grimes cried and blubbered on, his own tears did what his mother's could not do, and Tom's could not do, and nobody's on earth could do for him; for they washed the soot off his face and off his clothes; and then they washed the mortar away from between the bricks; and the chimney crumbled down; and Grimes began to get out of it.

Up jumped the truncheon, and was going to hit him on the crown a tremendous thump, and drive him down again like a cork into a bottle. But the strange lady put it aside.

"Will you obey me if I give you a chance?"

"As you please, ma'am. You're stronger than me—that I know too well, and wiser than me, I know too well also. And, as for being my own master, I've fared ill enough with that as yet. So whatever your ladyship pleases to order me; for I'm beat, and that's the truth."

"Be it so then—you may come out. But

264

remember, disobey me again, and into a worse place still you go."

"I beg pardon, ma'am, but I never disobeyed you that I know of.  I never had the honour of setting eyes upon you till I came to these ugly quarters."

"Never saw me?  Who said to you, Those that will be foul, foul they will be?"

Grimes looked up; and Tom looked up too; for the voice was that of the Irishwoman who met them the day that they went out together to Harthover.  "I gave you your warning then: but you gave it yourself a thousand times before and since.  Every bad word that you said—every cruel and mean thing that you did—every time that you got tipsy—every day that you went dirty—you were disobeying me, whether you knew it or not."

"If I'd only known, ma'am——"

"You knew well enough that you were disobeying something, though you did not know it was me.  But come out and take your chance. Perhaps it may be your last."

So Grimes stepped out of the chimney, and really, if it had not been for the scars on his face, he looked as clean and respectable as a master-sweep need look.

"Take him away," said she to the truncheon, "and give him his ticket-of-leave."

"And what is he to do, ma'am?"

"Get him to sweep out the crater of Etna; he will find some very steady men working out their time there, who will teach him his business: but mind, if that crater gets choked again, and there is an earthquake in consequence, bring them all to me, and I shall investigate the case very severely."

So the truncheon marched off Mr. Grimes, looking as meek as a drowned worm.

And for aught I know, or do not know, he is sweeping the crater of Etna to this very day.

"And now," said the fairy to Tom, "your work here is done. You may as well go back again."

"I should be glad enough to go," said Tom, "but how am I to get up that great hole again, now the steam has stopped blowing?"

"I will take you up the backstairs: but I must bandage your eyes first; for I never allow anybody to see those backstairs of mine."

"I am sure I shall not tell anybody about them, ma'am, if you bid me not."

"Aha! So you think, my little man. But you would soon forget your promise if you got back into the land-world. For, if people only once found out that you had been up my backstairs, you would have all the fine ladies kneeling to you, and the rich men emptying their purses before you, and statesmen offering you place and power; and young and old, rich and poor, crying to you, 'Only tell us the great backstairs secret, and we will be your slaves; we will make you lord, king, emperor, bishop, archbishop, pope, if you like—only tell us the secret of the backstairs. For thousands of years we have been paying, and

petting, and obeying, and worshipping quacks who
told us they had the key of the backstairs, and
could smuggle us up them; and in spite of all our
disappointments, we will honour, and glorify, and
adore, and beatify, and translate, and apotheotise
you likewise, on the chance of your knowing
something about the backstairs, that we may all go
on pilgrimage to it; and, even if we cannot get
up it, lie at the foot of it, and cry—

'   *Oh, backstairs,*
*precious backstairs,*
*invaluable backstairs,*          *comfortable backstairs,*
*requisite backstairs,*           *humane backstairs,*
*necessary backstairs,*           *reasonable backstairs,*
*good-natured backstairs,*        *long-sought backstairs,*
*cosmopolitan backstairs,*        *coveted backstairs,*
*comprehensive backstairs,*       *aristocratic backstairs,*
*accommodating backstairs,*       *respectable backstairs,*
*well-bred backstairs,*           *gentlemanlike backstairs,*
*commercial backstairs,*          *ladylike backstairs,*
*economical backstairs,*          *orthodox backstairs,*
*practical backstairs,*           *probable backstairs,*
*logical backstairs,*             *credible backstairs,*
*deductive backstairs,*           *demonstrable backstairs,*
                                  *irrefragable backstairs,*
          *potent backstairs,*
    *all-but-omnipotent backstairs,*
              *&c.*

Save us from the consequences of our own actions,
and from the cruel fairy, Mrs. Bedonebyasyoudid!'   Do not you think that you would be

a little tempted then to tell what you know, laddie?"

Tom thought so certainly. "But why do they want so to know about the backstairs?" asked he, being a little frightened at the long words, and not understanding them the least; as, indeed, he was not meant to do, or you either.

"That I shall not tell you. I never put things into little folks' heads which are but too likely to come there of themselves. So come—now I must bandage your eyes." So she tied the bandage on his eyes with one hand, and with the other she took it off.

"Now," she said, "you are safe up the stairs." Tom opened his eyes very wide, and his mouth too; for he had not, as he thought, moved a single step. But, when he looked round him, there could be no doubt that he was safe up the backstairs, whatsoever they may be, which no man is going to tell you, for the plain reason that no man knows.

The first thing which Tom saw was the black cedars, high and sharp against the rosy dawn; and St. Brandan's Isle reflected double in the still broad silver sea. The wind sang softly in the cedars, and the water sang among the caves: the sea-birds sang as they streamed out into the ocean, and the land-birds as they built among the boughs; and the air was so full of song that it stirred St. Brandan and his hermits, as they slumbered in the shade; and they moved their good old lips, and sang their morning hymn amid their dreams. But among all the songs one came across the water more sweet and clear than all; for it was the song of a young girl's voice.

And what was the song which she sang?   Ah, my little man, I am too old to sing that song, and you too young to understand it.   But have patience, and keep your eye single, and your hands clean, and you will learn some day to sing it yourself, without needing any man to teach you.

And as Tom neared the island, there sat upon a rock the most graceful creature that ever was seen, looking down, with her chin upon her hand, and paddling with her feet in the water.   And when they came to her she looked up, and behold it was Ellie.

"Oh, Miss Ellie," said he, "how you are grown!"

"Oh, Tom," said she, "how you are grown too!"

And no wonder; they were both quite grown up—he into a tall man, and she into a beautiful woman.

"Perhaps I may be grown," she said.   "I have had time enough; for I have been sitting here waiting for you many a hundred years, till I thought you were never coming."

"Many a hundred years?" thought Tom; but he had seen so much in his travels that he had quite given up being astonished; and, indeed, he could think of nothing but Ellie.   So he stood and looked at Ellie, and Ellie looked at him; and they liked the employment so much that they stood and

looked for seven years more, and neither spoke nor
stirred.

At last they heard the fairy say: "Attention,
children. Are you never going to look at me
again?"

"We have been looking at you all this while,"
they said. And so they thought they had been.

"Then look at me once more," said she.

They looked—and both of them cried out at
once, "Oh, who are you, after all?"

"You are our dear Mrs. Doasyouwouldbedoneby."

"No, you are good Mrs. Bedonebyasyoudid;
but you are grown quite beautiful now!"

"To you," said the fairy. "But look again."

"You are Mother Carey," said Tom, in a very
low, solemn voice; for he had found out something
which made him very happy, and yet frightened
him more than all that he had ever seen.

"But you are grown quite young again."

"To you," said the fairy. "Look again."

"You are the Irishwoman who met me the
day I went to Harthover!"

And when they looked she was neither of them,
and yet all of them at once.

"My name is written in my eyes, if you have
eyes to see it there."

And they looked into her great, deep, soft eyes,
and they changed again and again into every hue,
as the light changes in a diamond.

"Now read my name," said she, at last.

And her eyes flashed, for one moment, clear,

white, blazing light: but the children could not
read her name; for they were dazzled, and hid
their faces in their hands.

"Not yet, young things, not yet," said she,
smiling; and then she turned to Ellie.

"You may take him home with you now on
Sundays, Ellie.  He has won his spurs in the great
battle, and become fit to go with you and be a
man; because he has done the thing he did not
like."

So Tom went home with Ellie on Sundays,
and sometimes on week-days, too; and he is now
a great man of science, and can plan railroads, and
steam-engines, and electric telegraphs, and rifled
guns, and so forth; and knows everything about
everything, except why a hen's egg don't turn
into a crocodile, and two or three other little things
which no one will know till the coming of the
Cocqcigrues.  And all this from what he learnt
when he was a water-baby, underneath the sea.

"And of course Tom married Ellie?"

My dear child, what a silly notion!  Don't
you know that no one ever marries in a fairy tale,
under the rank of a prince or a princess?

"And Tom's dog?"

Oh, you may see him any clear night in July;
for the old dog-star was so worn out by the last
three hot summers that there have been no dog-
days since; so that they had to take him down and
put Tom's dog up in his place.  Therefore, as new
brooms sweep clean, we may hope for some warm
weather this year.  And that is the end of my story.

## MORAL

*And now, my dear little man, what should we learn from this parable?*

*We should learn thirty-seven or thirty-nine things, I am not exactly sure which: but one thing, at least, we may learn, and that is this—when we see efts in the pond, never to throw stones at them, or catch them with crooked pins, or put them into vivariums with stickle-backs, that the sticklebacks may prick them in their poor little stomachs, and make them jump out of the glass into somebody's work-box, and so come to a bad end. For these efts are nothing else but the water-babies who are stupid and dirty, and will not learn their lessons and keep themselves clean; and, therefore (as comparative anatomists will tell you fifty years hence, though they are not learned enough to tell you now), their skulls grow flat, their jaws grow out, and their brains grow small, and their tails grow long, and they lose all their ribs (which I am sure you would not like to do), and their skins grow dirty and spotted, and they never get into the clear rivers, much less into the great wide sea, but hang about in dirty ponds, and live in the mud, and eat worms, as they deserve to do.*

*But that is no reason why you should ill-use them:
but only why you should pity them, and be kind to them,
and hope that some day they will wake up, and be
ashamed of their nasty, dirty, lazy, stupid life, and try
to amend, and become something better once more.  For,
perhaps, if they do so, then after 379,423 years, nine
months, thirteen days, two hours, and twenty-one minutes
(for aught that appears to the contrary), if they work
very hard and wash very hard all that time, their brains
may grow bigger, and their jaws grow smaller, and
their ribs come back, and their tails wither off, and they
will turn into water-babies again, and perhaps after
that into land-babies; and after that perhaps into
grown men.*

*You know they won't?  Very well, I daresay you
know best.  But you see, some folks have a great liking
for those poor little efts.  They never did anybody any
harm, or could if they tried; and their only fault is,
that they do no good—any more than some thousands of
their betters.  But what with ducks, and what with
pike, and what with sticklebacks, and what with water-
beetles, and what with naughty boys, they are " sae sair
hadden doun," as the Scotsmen say, that it is a wonder
how they live; and some folks can't help hoping, with
good Bishop Butler, that they may have another chance,
to make things fair and even, somewhere, somewhen,
somehow.*

*Meanwhile, do you learn your lessons, and thank
God that you have plenty of cold water to wash in; and*

# DISTRIBUTORS
## *for Wordsworth Children's Classics*

**AUSTRALIA, BRUNEI & MALAYSIA**

Reed Editions
22 Salmon Street
Port Melbourne
Vic 3207
Australia

Tel: (03) 646 6716
Fax: (03) 646 6925

**GERMANY, AUSTRIA & SWITZERLAND**

Swan Buch-Marketing GmbH
Goldscheuerstraße 16
D-7640 Kehl am Rhein
Germany

**GREAT BRITAIN & IRELAND**

Wordsworth Editions Ltd
Cumberland House
Crib Street
Ware
Hertfordshire SG12 9ET

**INDIA**

Om Book Service
1690 First Floor
Nai Sarak, Delhi - 110006

Tel: 3279823/3265303
Fax: 3278091

**NEW ZEALAND**

Whitcoulls Limited
Private Bag 92098, Auckland

**SINGAPORE**

Book Station
18 Leo Drive
Singapore

Tel: 4511998
Fax: 4529188

**USA, CANADA & MEXICO**

Universal Sales & Marketing
230 Fifth Avenue
Suite 1212
New York, NY 10001 USA

Tel: 212-481-3500
Fax: 212-481-3534

**ITALY**

Magis Books
Piazza della Vittoria 1/C
42100 Reggio Emilia

Tel: 0522-452303
Fax: 0522-452845